# Contents

# 1. Showing off wife

This is a story that happened about 10 years ago. I have always had a burning desire to watch another guy see my wife Kathy naked. I tried for years to make it happen but was never successful. She had no interest. She was more or less a prude. My wife at the time was about 5ft tall and 140 pounds, nice soft skin, 36D boobs,, and a nice moderately furry pussy. So to cut to the chase after years of pleading and begging she agreed as long as it was in a hotel room, and with a stranger. Her ground rules were very clear. He was to remain fully clothed and he could only touch above the waist. I eagerly agreed to her terms. I posted an ad online and sorted through hundreds of replies. Finally I picked one. His name was Robert. We made arrangements and booked a hotel room in a nearby town. On the appointed evening I took my wife to the hotel, gave her a nice long bath and had her wait in the room. She was nervous as hell. I went down to the lobby to meet Robert. We reviewed the rules she had set and he agreed. I had given Kathy a few rules too. She would have to meet him at the hotel room door completely nude, and would have to remain nude the whole time he was there. We had also rehearsed every position and pose that I would ask her to do so there would be no surprises. I told Robert to wait for 5 minutes and then go up to the room. I hurried upstairs to get Kathy ready. For 5 long minutes she stood there naked, almost trembling waiting for the knock on the door. When he finally knocked, she looked at me with a "do I have to" look but I nodded yes, she had agreed already. She opened the door and let him in. There she stood in all her glory, full frontal nude as he stared at her body. I told her to give him a hug and told him it was ok to gently touch her breasts. They sat on the couch together trying to make small talk as he fondled her breasts and belly. I was excited beyond belief. I told her to get up and get him a beer that we had brought, so she had to walk around the room as he looked. Next I had her lay on the bed, legs spread wide while he sat between her legs getting an unclose look at her spread pussy. Finally I had her get on her hands and knees for a perfect rear view of everything, just as we had earlier rehearsed. I stretched the rules and let him hold her butt cheeks wide open. He got behind her and studied every detail of her pussy and rosebud. Then (again as I had agreed with Kathy), I told him it was time to leave. He told me what a great time he had had. Kathy, still completely nude, escorted him to the door, and gave him a very intimate hug, As soon as the door closed, I hugged and thanked Kathy for being so brave and accommodating and we had some incredible sex.

# 2. Fun on business trip

I am a 47 year old married guy from Atlanta, the wife and I have an open-ish relationship, and by ish, I mean we have discussed it but nothing has happened...until last week.

Last week I was traveling with one of our sales guys visiting customers and the first day was just me and him. The second day we picked up one of our account managers that I work fairly closely with in the office every day and she and I often go to lunch together and casually flirt, but nothing serious. The plan was for her to meet some of the customers she supports on Wednesday and Thursday and fly back home Thursday afternoon.

Tuesday night, we pick her up and go to dinner and head back to the hotel. After we get back, I get a text that she is having problems logging into our VPN and asks if I can come help her (we both had a few drinks at dinner). I am wearing basketball shorts and a T-shirt and she opens the door wearing a long nightshirt, and says "I have never seen you this casual before" to which I say the same to her. She tells me she is still getting ready for bed and points me to her computer. I sit down, and start trying to figure out why she can't connect while she goes back into the bathroom and closes the door. I figure out she isn't getting connected because the room is in my name (she doesn't travel much and doesn't have a corporate card), get her connected and just as I am about to get up, she comes out of the bathroom wearing just a towel.

My jaw hits the floor, I knew she had a nice body, but had no idea her tits were as big as they were since she wears baggy tops in the office and her butt is usually covered by them. She kind of grins and asks if I approve of her towel...I kind of stammer that I seem over dressed now and she says she has been thinking about this since we scheduled the trip and hopes that she isn't being to forward. I stammer something stupid I am sure and stand up and take off my shirt. She drops her towel and I am almost instantly hard. She is not just hot for 46 years old, but she is hot for any age. She has a nice body, definitely a mom ass, and while her stomach is not flat, it is still nice, but her tits are amazing...and natural (I later find out they are 34JJ).

She walks over to me and we start kissing hard and deep, she has the softest lips and her tongue is dancing with my tongue in each other's mouths...she pulls my shorts down and starts stroking me as I run my hands over her body.

She breaks the kiss and lays back on her bed and I climb in next to her and start sucking on her nipples and fingering her, she is soaked as I start kissing down her stomach and all around her inner thighs and the outer lips of her pussy before spreading her lips and licking her clit. She moans and tells me how good it feels as I slip a finger inside her and start fingering her as I lick her clit...it doesn't take long for her to explode.

After she calms down she pulls me up between her legs and guides me into her. I slowly start pumping in and out and while I would like to say I lasted 10 minutes and made her cum multiple times, I made it maybe 5 minutes before I unloaded inside her. She pulled my face down to her and kissed me deeply and said roll off of me and I will clean us up. She went into the bathroom, cleaned herself up and came back with a warm wet towel and cleaned me up. She said "oh good you are still hard" and climbed on top of me and slowly rode me for a solid 30 minutes cumming at least twice before she said she was tired and lay next to me as we drifted off to sleep.

The next morning I snuck back to my room hoping the sales guy didn't notice and we visited customers all day. Nothing was said about the night before at all during the day. The next night after dinner, I am back in my room and there is a knock on my door. I open it and she walks in and just starts kissing me, she basically rips off my clothes and pushes me back on the bed, she climbs on top of me and starts kissing me again and after a minute or two turns around and gets us in a hot 69...I love the taste of her and she is sucking me deep and hard, after she cums (which doesn't take long, she turns around and starts riding me, first laying on my chest grinding, then sitting up where I can play with her tits. She tells me she has never ridden a guy like this before, and loves the way it feels. She cums two more times riding me and ass if I am not enjoying it...I tell her I am very much but always struggle cumming while laying on my back...she rolls off of me and gets on her knees and says do me hard from behind....she didn't have to ask twice and I started fucking her hard and fast until I told her I was close...she begged me to fill her up and we both came together. Again we curled up, went to sleep and she got to sneak out so the sales guy didn't catch us.

The next morning we get up and visit a couple more customers then fly back together and I had already offered to drive her home from the airport. So again nothing is said about the previous two nights, and we sit next to each other on the plane and she fell asleep on my shoulder. We get to her house and she asks if I want to come in for a minute, and as soon as we get inside, she tells her daughter to go and get some dinner for them and we are alone.

She tells me we don't have much time, but wants to have sex one more time before I leave so we both strip quickly, and lay on her bed...I finger her to a quick orgasm and then she pulls me between her legs and tells me to fuck her hard and fast and fill her up. I pump her for maybe 5 minutes before cumming and she kissed me goodbye.

Work this week has been interesting, we have had lunch and talked about the trip a bit, we are talking about getting together one night next week to have some more fun!

# 3. Another encounter in a casino

This was at a local casino. She was dressed in a brown thin material dress that clung to her curvy plump huge tits and body. No Bra and no panties.

When we valeted the car the valet opened her door to let her, out of course she gave them a show unknowingly the dress went up I could tell the valet saw her exposed pussy, when she stood up her tits were almost falling out when she tucked them back in she would pull her dress out to get those puppies back in nipples and all were exposed,. As we walked in all could see her tits swaying back and forth. We stood in line to pull some money guys and woman were looking at her went to seek a slot machine the same thing; I walked behind her so the guys wouldn't think I was with her.

She sat at a slot that was a bar and she had to sit on a stool. Again the dress slid up the guy next to her was impressed. She was there for a bit the guy next to her made conversation with her they talked back and forth he bought her a drink little by little he touched her on the arm then he put his hand on her thigh, slowly it started moving up. I was sitting next to her like I didn't know her. More drinks. He kept telling her how gorgeous she looked in that dress. He then asked her are your breast real her respond was of course go head and feel them, sure enough he did then she looked at me you can feel them too, so I did. I said oh yea they're real, and then the guy took another feel held them for a bit. After a while she started to get up her favorite thing is spreading her legs when getting up as she is getting up she says, well I need to go find my husband, thanked him for the drinks and kissed him on the lips and he took one more feel of her tits. About this time she seemed pretty wobbly, found a machine she wanted there was 4 very young Mexican guys sitting around one guy playing, she asked one of them that wasn't playing if he was playing if not can she play, he got up stood behind the one playing another one sat next to her and started playing. So she was surrounded by these guys, I was on the other side of them, they were keeping an eye on her as she settled into her chair, yep up went the dress they looked at each other, they were talking in Spanish, mind U I'm Hispanic know some Spanish, she is Italian. Any way as she is settling her tits are swaying back and forth and her legs are opening. She starts playing, these guys are not paying attention to their machine just eyeing my wife the light from the machine allowed her dress to be see threw, the breast were very visible nipples and the whole tit. I didn't know how to start the seduction so I told her to turn so they can see up, they looked at me and asked me is she yours? In Spanish, I said yes in Spanish I said if you massage her shoulders she might want to fuck U guys, awkward but it worked. She turned so they could see her pussy and one of them started rubbing her shoulders. One guy bent over to look up her dress the one rubbing her went under her arms and cupped her breast, the others looked with amazement.

So I said to them "want to give her a massage", they said sure U have a room I said no we have a Motorhome. One said "all of us "I said yea. We never had 4 guys, this was getting really hot so was she. I said to her U ready? She said all of them? One guy said in Spanish no just 2 of us. So she got up her ass was right in front of one guy I believe he was the more dominate one. He pretended to lick her ass. Off we went they stayed behind her to watch her ass jiggle and in the light U could see the crack of her ass...

We got to the Motorhome I told one guy grab her ass and help her in he did, when we got in the dominate one got behind her and went under her arm and grab her tits, he slid her dress down and he cupped her breasts. As they got into the bed he sucked her nipples. She lay on her back removed her dress and spread her legs the other guy crawled between her legs, he had the bigger cock, he pulled the blanket over he didn't want to be taped.

They were very nervous, I think they were virgins.

He started to enter her she guided him in he stopped she grabbed his ass and pulled him in till he reached bottom he slowly retracted and she said "fuck me"!!, 3 times. I don't think he under stood so I told his friend tell him to fuck her, he went to his behind and pushed him in a couple of times and told him "dale con fuerte" do her hard. He rammed her and after a few strokes he cummed. So the other guy climbed on her and stuck his cock in her and fucked her a few times, he pulled out and started rubbing her body all over and fingered her clit she squirmed and cummed, he then put his cock in to her pussy and fucked her. She said man he has a hard cock. He continued to fuck her she was super wet U could hear the slosh like she always does when she is super turned on. She told me I want to suck his cock, I told him what she said so they got in a 69 position, and she swallowed his cock and gave him one of her master full BJs. She tunged his cock up and down the shaft of his cock, she went up his cock then slipped his cock into her mouth very slowly then took it all the way to her throat she likes, then start going up and down all the way to his balls she cupped his balls and pushed them up when she came down to the base of his cocks she tried to push his balls into her mouth then sped up sucking his cock went faster he lifted his ass putting his cock deeper into her throat he then let out a heavy grunt holding his cock in her throat as he cummed.

# 4. BBC had her hanging on

We were bored and wanting to party and didn't have the time for a long weekend. So we drove to Fayetteville N.C. to a house party to seek out our adventure. We arrived about 9 pm and mingled with everyone. What few people there were a good mixture of people and a few single men and only ONE gentleman of color? Seems most had connected with others already and had left or so I was told anyhow. So the wife and I sat down on the couch and I made sure she sat in the middle. This man sat beside her and introduced himself. Small chat while watching interracial porn on the TV and he made the remark of wanting to get with a white lady sometime. I told him to chat it up with people and see. He remarked that he tried but all seemed distant and non responsive. The wife is breathing a little heavy her eyes are glued to the white woman getting slammed like a screen door in a hurricane by a BBC and she commented that it "must be nice". So she leaning in on me and rubbing my leg so I eased her skirt up so he could see her ass. I caressed her and motioned him to join and he did so gladly. The three of us slipped off to one of the bedrooms and in moments she was moaning in delight and hanging on to the headboard and whimpering as he pounded her relentless. Soon we had and audience. If anyone else hooked up there that night I am not aware of it. We never went back.

# 5. A Not So Good Wife

I have to preface this with a few things about myself. I was a late bloomer, repressed, afraid. And the sex in my marriage died a hard death and when I tried to talk about it with my husband he told me, "Ask your friends, you'll see they don't have a sex life either." And so I asked my friends and my husband was very, very wrong. And then I meet this man. And he became my lover. And everything changed.

A few times a year my lover goes on a golf trip for a night or two with his buddies. This year they weren't too far away and he invited me to come down. I didn't take him serious at first. We're incredibly discreet about being seen together and who knows. But he asked again and was very clear "No shenanigans, just come meet me for dinner." It turned out I was home alone that weekend and so I decided to make the drive. I put on something cute and a pair of heels, and as always when I meet my lover, sexy panties. I wanted to feel sexy even if there would be no "shenanigans".

When I got to the hotel/resort I was met by my lover and his friend Zan. Zan and I have never met. However, we've spoken on the phone. As in while my lover and I are laying naked together my lover will call Zan and hand me the phone. I then tell Zan what it is I want, my lover's cock, my lover's cum. How I love to swallow, how I love the taste of my lover's cum. How I love to suck his cock, smooth and hard in my mouth while I lay on my belly, my legs and feet swaying back and forth in the air. How I crave his cock inside me, deep and warm. How I beg to be sent home fucked and filled. I say all of this to Zan as my lover and I fuck, so Zan can hear the rise and fall in my voice as I get more excited, as my clit, my whole body awakens. Somewhere along the way my lover hangs up and we tune out everything but our two bodies, skin on skin, pure pleasure. So Zan and I weren't strangers but yet, in a sense we were.

We went to the restaurant and had a delicious meal the three of us. We didn't talk sex, the conversation flowed easily and we laughed at each other. It was just three people sitting at a table sharing a meal, sharing a few drinks. Yet below the surface, all three of us were turned on by the secret between us.

After dinner we walked around a bit and they had a drink and I thought I should head home and told my lover that. "No," he told me, "I have a surprise in the room for you." And I laughed and said, "I bet". But he asked me to come upstairs, sweet as can be and promised no shenanigans. Now the thought of shenanigans, the possibility of it was a turn on for me. This energy from two men all to myself, even over dinner wasn't lost on me. So part of me believed him and part of me knew that together in a hotel room the "hands to ourselves" couldn't last. The whole night we had not so much as touched. When I'm near him physically I have a deep desire to be closer. For his tongue to run along my lip. For his fingers to seek out my nipples. I crave his skin on mine. To feel the softness of his hair between my fingers. So the whole night was this beautiful torture. So close and yet so off limits. On the elevator ride up I was both calm and nervous staring at the three of us in the floor to ceiling mirrors.

When got to the room there was that moment of awkwardness as we shuffled around. And then from the hotel fridge came a chocolate mousse cake, a late birthday surprise-candles and all. And they sang an out of tune, funny "Happy Birthday" to me and we all laughed. My lover cut me a piece and I sat on the bed, surrounded with fluffy pillows my toes tucked under the covers eating a delicious piece of cake, happy.

My lover came and lay next to me. He turned on the television and I did what I always do when he's close. I start to smell his neck and kiss his chin line and fold my body into the crevice between his arm and his body. I love his body. Every part of it

Strong, Steady. He has the body of a man who can move the earth.

And I knew of coarse that Zan was there. Sitting at the desk chair just across the room. Eating my birthday cake watching the two of us. And it took me a moment to let go of all the old bullshit, the guilt, the shame and see what was unfolding as three adults playing out a fantasy together. Three adults with sexual appetites that only increased when mingled together. And my lover searched my face for any fear, any cause to pull away and stop but only found my growing enthusiasm.

My lover moved my hand over his cock, still in his pants. And I stroked him until that incredible feeling of his cock getting harder from my touch. And then I did what I never could have done a year ago. I sat up on my knees and slid down the bed to unzip his pants and take his hard cock in my mouth. First I rubbed my lips on it through his boxers and then I slid down his boxers and watched his cock spring upright, slid off his pants and boxers and took him in my mouth.

My husband hates when I make noise during sex. My lover, not so much. He lets me squeal and hum and make happy sighs. He wants to hear me enjoying myself, wants to hear me enjoying him.

Than I did something that I never thought I had the nerve to do. The freedom to do. I slid off the bed and stood in front of my lover and Zan. I was wearing a jumper and I pulled it down in one easy movement, standing in my bra and panties. I looked over and Zan had taken his pants off. His cock was in his hand, pulled through the front flap of his boxers. He was hard, stroking his cock up and down as he watched me. And my lover lay on the bed, his shirt off now, naked and longing. I felt this sense of freedom I have never felt before. Empowered. I don't desire Zan. I only wanted my lover but his presence there, his eyes fixed on me was a thrill I'd never come close to experiencing.

I took off my bra and eased off my panties, climbed back onto the bed and went for what I desire most, my lovers cock in my mouth. There's something erotic and yet soothing about burying my head deep in his cock and balls, Tasting him, Feeling the warmth of his balls against my face. I put his cock in my mouth and slid my finger under his balls, my nail gently adding pressure underneath. I sucked and licked and ran my tongue along the seam of his balls until he pulled me up and drove his cock inside me. My lover flipped me over and took me from on top, positioning us so that Zan had a better view. And Zan came to the bed, his cock out hard, desperate to join us. But my lover told him to sit on the edge of the other bed. That night he could only watch. And although he was disappointed, he was willing to do whatever it took to stay there beside us.

I begged my lover to cum inside me; I pulled him deeper until I felt that first rush of pre-cum. I begged him and begged him to fill me because when I'm near him I desire that more than anything.

Nothing satisfies me like the feeling of my lover losing control and giving me every last bit of his cum. From his body to mine.

Nothing else is as satisfying.

Our bodies are made for each other.

Later, Zan told us "I came so hard I wanted to scream out but I was afraid I'd screw up your rhythm."

There will be another time. Another man there to watch us. Because I want that feeling again of stripping down and two men, hard, watching me. And because what my lover does to me, how he fulfills all my fantasies deserves to be shared.

I giggle every time someone says "shenanigans" and I can never eat a chocolate mousse cake without thinking of my lover moving my hand over his hard cock and me, looking over my shoulder and seeing another man there, eyes on me.

For my lover, I am grateful.

# 6. Her first threesome (that I know of!)

So I wrote before and did not know if it actually happened or not and now I know it did I'm writing the details cause it's too good not to....we had been out for a nice dinner - just the two of us - and had to be back for the sitter by 11. Everything was going well until our stroll home. It was a nice balmy NY night but then we had an argument about something ridiculous (isn't it always). She stormed off (it was my fault and I knew it) and I knew I had to go home to relieve the sitter. I woke up at 2am but no sign, 5am still no sign, 7am kids got up but still no sign and I'm beginning to get worried when at 915am in she sheepishly walks. We leave it there and don't talk all day. Once kids were down my wife goes to bed and shortly after I get a text 'come in'. And she immediately says I had a threesome last night so let's get this out of the way........and here's how it went (me uber curious and acting mad)

She goes to a bar, thinks the barman is cute. He's 22 and knows all the hotties. My wife sees this as a challenge. She's drinking prosecco and he's keeping her glass full, chatting away and flirting. Can't believe you're 38 etc. Do you have a girlfriend all that nonsense. Then he says I have some favors if you want to party, follow me to the bathroom. She says she has no cash he says it'll only cost a kiss. So she starts kissing him and doing lines with him rest of the night. Eventually closing time, she's now his. He grabs a bottle from the bar and says come back with me. I live with a roommate I used to play football with on Lower East Side. She goes back and they start kissing on the sofa, she's grabbing his crotch but not loads of action there. She gets him to unzip her dress and she's standing there in heels, black stockings, little black knicker shorts and a black bra, her boobs pushed tight. They are kissing and he's rubbing her through her underwear and she's getting very wet. She takes his shirt off and he's pretty ripped she says and starts to put her hand into his pants which are also now wet but there is not much in terms of hardness. She takes off her knickershorts and just then his roommate arrives back. He is initially flustered but she says relax and brings the first guy by the hand into a room. She continues kissing him and takes her bra off then she goes down on him and there is still a lot of floppyness. So pissed off and wearing just her stockings she opens the door and asks his friend who is in the kitchen what his name is. He stutters Timmy (she thinks!) and she says Timmy come in here and fuck me right now......Timmy looks at his buddy (Brian) who shrugs

So in comes Timmy who has not done coke and his dick is already almost coming through his jeans. You want to fuck a milf she says and starts opening his jeans. He's a little shorter (like (6-2) and nervous. She pulls off his t-shirt and starts kissing him. Then his jeans and then she shows him her bling on her left hand and says see a milf. She starts stroking his dick and the poor guy like cums there and then. She wipes him up with his t-shirt and starts sucking his dick and balls....then she pushes him on the bed and sits cowgirl on him and starts fucking him. Leaning back and letting him grab her tits and then leaning forward so he can suck her nipples which are rock hard

When he comes again, better this time like 6/7 minutes, she gets off him and goes to the kitchen (tiny apartment) so it's like right there and leans down to do a line. As she's doing so she says she feels somebody come up behind her - the original barman who has been watching all this and he jams a much bigger cock into her from behind. A bigger hard cock! And he starts fucking her until he too comes about 10 minutes later (finally a yeah for coke!).

When she's done she goes back in and lies on the bed and Timmy asks if he can go again. Hell ya she says and turns over for him to fuck her doggy. At the same time first guy sticks his dick in her mouth and they spit toast her. Then they swap and this goes on a while till she says she must have fallen asleep eventually. She wakes up and realizes it's 730am! And she's in trouble! She grabs her things, kisses them both (she says they were defo awake but pretending to sleep) and leaves.

I was mad at first but find it all so incredibly hot I can't stay mad. And we still fantasize about it all the time! Oh well

# 7. Wife 1st time with someone else

I have had the fantasy of seeing my wife with another man, well awhile back I told her my fantasy and she wasn't as shocked as I thought she would be. From then on everytime we were having sex or she was jacking me off she would talk about some guys at work flirting with her and wanting to fuck her. I would cum so hard and she would just smile and say that didn't take long. And when I would use her dildos on her and tell her it was the guy's from work fucking her she would cum really hard and usually squirt. I asked her who it was and was she really thinking about going further with them. She told me 1 was a black guy (Mark) and the other was a white guy (James) and both were in their mid twenties and lived together. Mark works in the same area as her and always flirting and talking dirty to her. Many times she would come home and would be so horny. She asked me what I wanted her to do and I told her I was good with whatever she wanted to do. She wasn't sure they were serious since she's 50, but I told her if they weren't interested that they wouldn't be flirting with her. So tonight they were having trouble with the machines in her area and had to work over several hours. She called me around 3 p.m. and told me she would be staying over and didn't know what time she would be home. And Mark and James were working with her. I told her to flirt with them and do whatever they wanted her to do. She said she would think about it. About an hour later she text me and told me they were hitting on her pretty hard and James asked her if she wanted to bet on something and the loser had to do whatever the winner asked. She agreed and he told her that the bet was what color panties she had on. Mark guessed blue and James guessed black. Mark was right and he told her that at break he wanted her to go to the bathroom and take her panties off and give them to him. She text me and asked me what she should do and I told her a bet is a bet. At 5 she went to break and took her panties off and gave them to Mark. She said he handed them to James and told him to smell that sweet pussy. From there on the talk got dirtier and they told her they wanted to fuck her and she would want more. Around 7 she called me and told me all of this and I told her to do what she wanted just keep me informed. They asked her if she could give them a ride to their apartment up the street so they wouldn't have to walk, she agreed to do it. At 9 she called me and told me she was leaving work but had to drop the boys off before she headed home. She then told me she was so horny and had a wet spot on her pants. Luckily her pants were dark and her uniform shirt covered her crotch. I have never been so excited or so hard. The suspense was killing me. I got a text around 10 saying she would be home later, the text was from her phone but it also said thanks Mark. A little bit ago I got another text saying your wife is one hot slut. And they would be done with her shortly and they would be sending her home with a stretched, wore out pussy full of cum. She called me a few minutes ago and told me she was on her way home. And she had videos and other souvenirs for me.

# 8. Bajan Delights 3

I left of at that part in our history where Michelle had just let Josh into our hotel room. So she looked me straight between the eyes and said "some fantasies are best kept as fantasies and some are best lived out".

She then reached out to me with her soft hand and stroking the back of my hand smiled at me and said "I hope you don't mind darling but I invited Josh back here to give me a damn good fucking". Well what could I say? I could hardly object as I had been egging her on all holiday.

I said of course it was fine but was wondering what she had in mind as in - was I to join in or watch – she sensed my confusion. She invited Josh onto the bed and then came back towards me. She told me I could watch and kneel on the bed and touch her, kiss her, play with her tits but not to try to fuck her or get in their way. She was like a thing possessed and I was certainly to do what she said or fuck it up completely in which case she would either call a halt or kick me out.

I watched as she bent over the bed to kiss Josh full on the lips. As she bent forward I couldn't help but touch her arse as I looked at her soaking pussy. She immediately straightened up, turned to me and said quite sharply – "darling, I just told you the rules, I love you and adore you but know your place tonight". Fuck I had never seen her like this.

She turned away and reached down to Josh's boxers and his hard cock. I could see it was big but not really how big (they are always massive in these stories right?).

She was stroking him through his boxers and she moved to kiss him full on his lips and was kissing him for ages. My cock was so fucking stiff.

She stood once more and suggested I lay on the bed beside them. She peeled off her dress which was still quite clingy and her lovely huge breasts looked amazing in her lacy bra. Josh let out a gasp and said how he had noticed she had big titties but didn't realise how big. She peeled off the rest of her dress and unhooked her bra setting her titties free – she stood there completely naked having given me her knickers back at the club; her areolae were really puckered and her nipples hard. She climbed back on the bed and straddled Josh, dangling her tits in his face and rubbing her pussy on his cock through his boxers. She looked at Josh and told him how much she loved black cock then looked at me, smiled and whispered thank you darling.

I gently stroked her back and told her to make the most of him. She turned back to Josh and kissed him full on again, his hands were all over her arse, pulling her arse cheeks apart and scratching at her skin. She sat up and turning round started to kiss his boxers. She reached inside his shorts and pulled his cock out. He was not huge, probably about 8 inches but his cocked looked really angry and sexy as she placed her lips over his dark purple head. Such a sexy sight – in another world I could have sucked on that gorgeous knob head myself.

I was struggling to hold back and stick to her rules, my hands wandered along her body and I squeezed her hands a couple of times. She maneuvered her leg over Josh and planted her pussy right over his face – the poor fucker nearly drowned. His hands were on her arse and tongue firmly in her pussy. I didn't know which to enjoy most, her sucking his cock or him her pussy. I was wanking my own cock next to them both and desperate to have her. I reached out to her hand and tried to entice her to rub my cock but she pulled away and shot me a chastising glance.

She climbed off of Josh and I thought I had blown it but how wrong I was, she just rolled onto her back, slid her hands from her belly to her pussy mound and told Josh to fuck her.

Wow what a sight. Josh smiled at me then climbed between my wife's thighs but hesitated as his cock neared her pussy. He looked at me and asked "is this OK man?" I replied yes and then realised he was referring to fucking her bareback so I just said that she was in charge. She looked at me as if for reassurance and I just smiled. She reached down, grabbed Josh's cock and pulled him into her pussy again telling him to fuck her. He pushed deep in her and then began really fast and furious fucking – she was already heading to cumming I could tell and his pounding was pushing her over the edge. Her legs straightened and stiffened her breath was fast and shallow followed by deep breaths which she held then gasped. And then there it was, to say she exploded is an understatement and her belly was shaking and shuddering. Josh slowed down and lifted himself on his elbows, bending his head forward and kissing my wife so very passionately. I reached over and began to stroke her soft belly and could still feel it pulsing. Josh began long slow stroked in her. Not being able to stop myself I reached down to touch her pussy and could feel the hardness of Josh's cock against my little finger as well as how wet he and she were. I thought I was staying in the rules but when I touched her clitoris she froze solid, turned to look at me and said very harshly – what the fuck – I told you the rules now get your hand off my cunt.

I pulled my hand away and rolled away mouthing sorry to her.

She then continued saying - in fact, as you can't control yourself – get off the bed and go sit in the chair and watch as this lovely black cock fucks my soaking pussy. She was on fire.

She pushed Josh into the bed and straddled his cock, I watched as I saw him enter her – she was sooooo swollen and dripping wet. Josh wasted no time at all and was pounding up to meet her riding hips. He was pulling her arse cheeks apart again and I leaned sideways in the chair to get the best view – it was luck the best porn film I had ever watched.

Michelle kept looking over her shoulder at me, throwing her head back in extasy and clawing at Josh's chest as she rode him hard.

Suddenly she stopped and sat hard down on him, making him still for a few seconds.

She turned her head and shoulders towards me and told me I

could stand at the end of the bed and watch just how hard she was fucking Josh from close up. I did as she said and positioned myself at the end of the bed. I had never seen her so strong and so in control. She leaned forward and with her face next to Josh's she told him to fuck her hard and fast and pump his cum in her. Josh didn't need telling twice and he was fast and crazy within seconds. Michelle was leaning forward ovwer him and I could see her lovely arse and gaping pussy as his black cock pounded her. As I stood close I suddenly became aware of the aromas coming from her pussy – a sweet mix of her juices and his cock, mixed with earlier perspiration. Sweat was dripping along her back and her hair was soaked. Suddenly she sat bolt upright and started riding Josh like a horse – she was cumming again. As she came hard she fell forward. Josh resumed pounding her as she flopped forward then she was reaching back towards me with her hands as if trying to grab me, kind of wiggling her fingers for me to come nearer but I was hesitant given the earlier faux pas. Still flopped forward she turned her head towards me, her eyes were gone somewhere very far away, she was trying to say some-thing but the words were not coming, she was still cumming herself when she blurted out my name and told me to lick the fuck out of her arse. What the fuck, this was new territory even for us. I leant forward and with the aromas getting stronger, I grabbed her arse and pushed my tongue into her puckered hole. She was then telling me deeper and deeper and telling Josh to cum in her. He stiffened, locked his legs out and I could sense him pumping his seed deep in her hole.

When he finally relaxed, we all collapsed in a heap. Josh flat out on his back, Michelle sprawled across him flat and with her legs wide open and me with my face on her bum and the sweet smell of her pussy and arse in my nostrils.

We seemed to drift off into a semi sleep state for maybe half an hour or so. I awoke to the sound and sight of Michelle and Josh kissing. She was thanking him for an amazing time and gently suggesting it would be good for him to think about heading off. He didn't resist and extracting himself from below my wife, he slipped back into his boxers slipped into the bathroom and slipped out of the door a little while later.

As the door closed I rolled onto my back on the bed – Michelle lazily rolled a leg over me until she was straddling me. I thought I was finally going to get to fuck her but as I pushed my hardon towards her from below she shook her head. She said she was too sore and I would have to wait but then she moved forward just a little, sat up and lifted her hips just above my cock – she looked down, parted her lips a little with her hands and squeezed like she was going to pee but instead she dripped a mix of her juices and Josh's cum all over my cock and belly and said it would still be there for me in the morning. She then lay down on me in the gooey mess and we fell off to sleep.

# 9. Past experiences

Do other wives get asked, by their husbands, about past experiences?

My hubby likes hearing about some of mine

I was an ugly duckling and when I was growing up
I was rather plump and not really pretty at all, but I had a close friend who looked rather similar and we got on ok.

She had been given a holiday as a present by her
mum and she took me with her to a holiday camp in Bognor

I guess we looked rather lonely to casual on-lookers, but she had "borrowed" some sex toys from her older sister, and we certainly made full use of them for the first few days, we never considered it as being "Lezzies", we were just helping each other out.

One evening we were chatted up by three older lads and to be honest we could hardly believe our luck

They bought us quite a few drinks and then suggested we went back to their chalet for a coffee.

After a few more drinks one of the lads took my friend into the back bedroom and I was left with the other two.

They were soon kissing and undressing me and I was excited, but also scared as they clearly assumed that I was experienced, when in fact, (apart from the dildos) I was very much a virgin and I had not even seen an erect cock, let alone stroked one.

I few moments later, I was naked and they were both kissing and

exploring me intimately as I lay
there enjoying the attention.

One of them placed my hand on his erection and I was fascinated by it and I was delighted to be
encouraged to kiss it and stroke it and admire it
and to lick it.

One of them licked me and I was in seventh heaven for ages and
I could have taken a lot more of that, but they were keen of
course for real sex.

It dint hurt as the first one eased his lovely wet cock into my
eager little pussy, thanks to all the practice I had had with my
friend's sex toys

It felt amazingly sexy as he pushed his beautiful manhood in
and out of me as I lath there enjoying every moment of this
grown up fun.

When he came in me I almost hit the roof and I remember them
saying how good I was.

It was so sexy also, for me, as he withdrew his slightly softening
cock and his friend eagerly took his place in my vacant pussy

I thought for a moment that he may not like using me with
his friends sperm still swimming around inside me, but f anything it made it even more erotic

He didn't last as long as his friend had, but they were soon showing me how a little sucking and stoking would make their wonderful cocks ready for use again, and again.

I could hardly walk back to our chalet later, I felt as if I had been
fucked senseless, and that was probably true, as I didn't give it a
thought, till the morning that I may have been made pregnant,
but luckily that didn't happen.

My friend and I compared details of course, and she was so

proud of me for handling two of them as my first time, apparently her lad had only lasted a moment or two and he went to sleep a few moments after, so I told her about how you are apparently supposed to "Suck them back to life"

and we giggled and chatted about it as we gently played with each other to help re-live our first time with real cocks

Sadly we didn't get chatted up again during that holiday and it was rather disappointing to note that the lads had moved on to slimmer, prettier girls, but at least we had been laid at last !

# 10. Her first bbc

My wife of 41 years recently had her first BBC. Karen is 66 and we have been in the lifestyle for almost 20 years .we have lived most if not all of our fantasies, however Karen was always shy about black guys, her being so pale skinned i always wanted to see the contrast.

Karen is 5 ft 2 about 150 lbs with little tits and a killer ass. I had decided to push the issue behind her back. I told her we were going to a hotel out of town, told her to shave herself and to pack her toys.... which included old stockings to tie her, blindfold. I told her she was going to be shared. She was excited at the idea went to get ready and off we went. She wanted to know who was going to have her and started to name her past lovers, I eventually told her he was a new lover that I had met, that got her very excited she just loves a new cock. I told her she was going to be tied and blindfolded, and would only see him after he saw her naked and after she had sucked his cock hard, told her she was going to be treated like a slut. I slide my hand up her skirt she was soaked.

We got to the hotel room had a glass of wine. I told her to open the curtains and get undressed, she did exactly has told removed her blouse and reveled her braless boobs then slipped off her skirt leaving just her stockings on. she looked so slutty i was harder than i had been in awhile. She asked if curtains were going to be open while she was being used, i said not this time, because being tied up I didn't want anyone seeing that and calling the cops. I asked her if anyone saw her she responded yes, told her to close the curtains get on the bed it was time to tie her up.

Have to finish this later thought I would have more time but people are coming to work

*11. 9 5*

We had been fighting. It started on the Thursday before our weekly date night on Saturday. Friday came and went without resolution remotely close, same with Saturday. I wrote her an email detailing my gripes. Then late Saturday afternoon we sat down and discussed my email.

Then discussion flowed, crying, much emotion, and review of our long marriage. Our love of each other shone tenderness very present.
She asked at 6 pm if we should go to bed. I said let's wait until a little later.

At 8 p.m. off we went to bed with the lecky blankets on 9. As most vividly know, pure heaven for naked bodies.

We were both ultra-hungry for each other. Embracing tightly, kissing quickly flowed into tonguing that was raw, driven, heavy, full-on, ultra-passionate..... sssssssss..... we could not get enough of each other's tongues...... this sending shivers through my body just thinking of it......

Then we flowed into around ten minutes of delicate slow caressing and massaging of her whole body...... particularly neck, shoulders, back and buttocks.... with lots of shudders and moans from her.

Then she moved onto her back...ohhhhh.....the fireworks immediately started as I caressed her breast tummy and thighs..... and ran my hand briefly over her vulva.... which immediately jangled my nerves as she already felt wet-wet. Driven now, my hand returned to her vulva lightly and slowly, but dramatically she was awash with wetness.

She had been in bed reading for close to 10 minutes before I arrived. My strong sense is she was highly aroused and masturbated, because her outer lips were wide open, both inner and outer liberally wet all over. When I slipped my finger between her lips, her vagina was wide-wide open, cavernous, my fingers going in onto her G spot with ease.

Ohhhhh I rubbed all her vulval lips with five fingers held together..... up and down, then circles.....she was so so wet, plus moving in the bed thrusting her hips and moaning. It drove me into inflamed passion. She was feverously in the hot zone moaning and groaning. I rubbed her oh so erect clit, sliding up and down her channel with ease, bumping across her oh so hard and erect clit. Then a finger to her G spot amidst a flood of juices ..... so so wet.

I had taken 50 mg of V one-hour before, resulting in my cock feeling ultra-long and thick and so hard. She was caressing it urgently, in a haze doing so, as well as rubbing my right nipple which she knows provides a powdery exquisite delicate flow of sensation.
We were now inside deep-deep driven passion, raw, hungry, unrestrained...ssssssssssssssssssss.

She asked for her current favorite vibrator...... applied it...... two minutes later a mighty cry and heavy jerking of her body as she came heavily.
I then presented my fortunately still hard cock to her entrance (many blessings to Viagra). We were in scissor position, she on her back, me sideways. The head pushed effortlessly into her slipperiness....and away we went fucking like rabbits.

Rhythmic to start with I concentrated on ensuring the head of my cock rubbed onto her G spot and vaginal roof as it made each thrust..... Also while thrusting I rubbed her still sublimely wet clit plus an alternating nipple at the same time trying to help maximise her sensations. Both her nipples were beautifully turgidly erect, areolas puckered…sssss….Earlier I had sucked each for several minutes minutes… moan… so sensual and erotic…… slurping, noisy, leaving tongue across slowly, sucking, razoring, gobbling, and blowing ohhhhh…….

We settled into a semi-urgent fucking until she urged me to go for it, oh we were moaning and groaning…… both surrendered to unrestrained passion…. until over I went…. came…and came…..
Looking at the clock, we had been at it for just over 30 minutes.

A vivid, powerful, heavy-duty, high-passion lovemaking, raw and raunchy, with a total and hungry surrender to sexual passion. 9.5/10

How wonderful two 80-year-olds can know such sparkling high-voltage sexual expression, wonder and delight. We are deeply blessed to have such a loving partnership after all these years.

P.S. the moral of this story - ensure you have a fight quite regularly to ensure high sexual passion!

# 12. Her ego gets her in into trouble.....

This is one of my wife's favorite adventures. We have been together since college, been open to some extent pretty much the whole time we have been together. We are in our late 40's now; this took place when she was around 30.

Mary worked for a retail management/real estate firm, good size. She enjoyed her work, good people. Yeah she played with a few of the men there, including her boss. Some with me involved, some alone.

Anyways, one of the guys in the office was engaged and they decided to have an after work, happy hour party for him a couple of weeks before he got married. It was planned for a Friday around 3, leave the office early, have a few drinks, laughs.

I drove Mary to work that day, she was going to ride with one of her female coworkers to and from the party. Knowing she would get a little buzz on and be in a good mood when she got home, she talked me into dropping the kids of at the grandparents for the night. She put on a sexy little set of blue bra and panties, a little shear, her favorite jeans that made her ass look great, nice button shirt.

Well it was a slow Friday, so they actually were all ready to leave the office by 1 so they headed over to start early. Nothing wild, some food, some drinks, lots of laughs, teasing the groom, nice fun.

Around 4 the place was getting really crowded as other offices in the area let out and people began to unwind. Some people started to leave to get home for their weekend, a few diehards about 10 guys, 3 gals were still hanging out. Place was too crowded, so the boss suggested they head to his house to continue and for dinner.

Mary rode with her boss as they stopped at a liquor store to pick up a few things, the other two gals road together, the guys whatever.

Well the other two gals forgetting they were Mary's ride home decided they wanted to go shopping instead and never showed. No biggie Mary knew she could call me or get a ride home from someone else. In fact she called to let me know where she was and she would be home in an hour or two.

The boss had a finished basement set up to entertain, wet bar, tables, big TV, nice music system. They got some pizza and wings. Cards were played, music, jokes, laughs, nothing out of control.

At one point a few others left, leaving Mary, her boss and about 6 other guys. Everyone was behaving appropriately.

Well suddenly, this one smart ass, will call him Jeff because I forget his name, pipes up "It is too bad Mary is still here we could have a sexy woman her to dance for the groom"

Well Mary was only slightly under the influence at this point, but she never liked someone getting one over on her, and liked to have the last word especially if she was drinking. Well in her mind she heard him saying he did not think she was sexy or could dance. He was not one of the guys she had ever played with.

So some back and forth started between them, her acting indigent about his perceived insult, him not backing down but trying to explain what he meant. Besides he added she wasn't brave enough to dance for them.

Well that was that, her ego saw RED. So she walked over turned up the music, grabbed a shot off the bar, then moved to an open area and began dancing. Now she told me her only intent was to dance around a bit for a song just to shut the guy up.

The guys laughed, cheered, as Mary danced around shaking her ass, nothing too dirty, she enjoyed the attention, but was not thinking any sexual thoughts.

Song ended, the guys clapped, she went back to the table to finish playing cards. Well a minute or two later Jeff being teased, pipes up again, that the dance was not what he meant, and the Mary was not brave enough to really dance.

Well, up she shot again, switched the radio from some mindless DJ chatter, and found "Bad to the Bone" just starting. Another shot and she was off on the dance floor, really shaking it, but again thinking more of just shutting Jeff up.

She shook it a little more, bent over some to show off her ass, guys teased Jeff, he then said, see she won't show anything.

Well with that Mary, undid a couple of buttons on her top, giving a little flash of cleavage and a hint of her blue bra.

The guys really cheered now, no rude comments, just asking her to shake it, etc. Someone did yell take it off, but they all took it as a joke.

Some banter back and forth between Jeff and Mary, nothing rude, nothing mean, they were just having good natured fun, got her dancing again.

This time a few singles were thrown at her, one or two tucked in the back pocket of her jeans. And yeah at this point she began to feel a bit sexy, but was thinking more of what fun she would have with me when she got home. As the guys encouraged her more, hooted, whistled, told her how great he ass looked, she got a bit more turned on.

At some point some buttons, those loose looped ones, came undone on her shirt and her shirt was open. When she noticed, she quickly pulled it closed, but some more singles thrown at her and calls to take it off. Then Jeff and another guy teasing she was too chicken.....well off the shirt came.

Thing is she had forgotten what bra she had one. Thinking in her head, that well it is just a bra, no different than a bathing suit top....well except this bra wa a bit shear, and so not only did the guys see her bra, they could see her nipples.

It took her a minute or so to realize whe the guys got so loud, but it was too late. She still was figuring at the end of the song, she would say enough and put her shirt on.

Well the song ended and before she could gather her shirt, she found herself at the bar, having another shot., laughing, enjoying the attention. Some hands touched her arm, back, felt nice, no groping.

Another song came on she really liked and she was back dancing again. No things were a bit more serious. She was feeling hotter, sexy, the guys were more vocal. Some more tips were given a few into her bra. Calls to take off more, and she found herself kicking off her shoes, then the crowd silenced as she undid her jean buttons and zipper.

She made a big show of shimmying out of them, bending over to give the guys in fron a good shot of cleavage and the guys in back a great view of her ass.

Well tips really started and now she was dancing FOR them, rubbing against them, tips were stuck into her panties, some right up front. She was getting wet. They guys could see through the back of her panties and a little in front. She also noticed that some of the guys were starting to swell.

Someone, probably Jeff, said she should give the groom a lap dance. They pushed him onto a couch, and Mary agreed but only for him, then she was done.

She worked her way to the groom, dancing as sexy as she could for him, shaking her tits in front of his face, bending her ass over at him. She straddled him, first facing the other guys, then turning around to sit straddling his lap. She teased him and let the guys know he was hard.

His hands were on her hips. But one slid down her ass between her legs, and he let the guys know how damp her panties were.

She grabbed his cock and told him his bride was a lucky woman. She went to get up as the song ended and looked around to see a group of horny guys around her all with obvious erections.

Some jokes were made about leaving the poor groom in such shape and a real dancer would relieve him. Her boss stepped in at this point and told the guys to relax a bit and that not a word of this was to be spoken to anyone not there.

He told Mary she could get dressed "if she wanted" the guys all begged for one more dance. So she did. Well now they were a bit more handy, nothing rough, but her tits got felt, as did her ass, someone tipping her managed to rub her clit briefly.

Well she went back to the groom to tease him some more and again calls were made to "help the poor guy" out. She stood up and danced against the boss facing the group, he slid a tip into the back of her bra and also unhooked her bra. She jumped away, trying to keep the bra on, but the cheers and encouragement of the guys, she let it fall to the floor.

Stunned silence, then wild cheers. She went back to the groom, sat on his lap and as she grinds on him a little he reached up and began rolling her nipples. At this point, she was gone. But she wanted to control things, so she said she would help the groom out, but then had to leave.

She slid onto the floor on her knees, and began undoing his jeans, she pulled them down, and exposing what she told me was a very sexy cock. Not too long, not too thick, the groom looked nervous. The other guys had gleems in their eyes. Her boss just smiled.

She played with his cock and balls, before leaning forward to kiss each ball, then trail her tongue up his cock, before swirling her tongue around his head tasting a bit of precum, then swallowing him whole. She became aware of some shouts from the crowd, but not sure what they were saying.

She loves giving head, and was soaking her panties. She knew she would probably cum sucking him off, and could not wait.

At some point she became aware that others were touching her ass, back. Someone even slid a finger in her pussy for a second, but she was focused on the delicious hard young cock in her mouth. She tasted more precum, he was rock hard, he groaned everytime she deep throated him, he was polite and did not fuck her mouth, letting her do the work.

She felt him tensing, she sucked harder, and faster, grabbing his ass, moaning loudly onto his cock. Orgasm starting to shake her body, which everyone had to be able to see. Suddenly the groom gasped, and his cum shot into her mouth, she held tight not letting a drop escape.

The guys went nuts. Cheering, calling her the best. As she continued to suck the grooms softening cock, she felt a few more hands on her, and then she realized her panties were pulled down and she looked around and saw everyone had their cocks out. A finger deftly worked her clit it was the boss.

At some point he had had someone grab a camping cushion out of the store room, it was spread on the floor, she found herself pulled to her feet.

She stood in the middle of the floor, surrounded by her co-workers, she was nude, she could taste the cock and cum of the groom, hands began to touch her. He neck and back were kissed, nipples pulled, twisted, sucked, multiple fingers played around he dripping pussy, no idea how many guys were trying to finger her nor how many actually were.

A finger slid into her ass, and she was gone, another orgasm shook her body and was held up by the guys, her hands found themselves full of cock. Then she was on her knees, first one cock then other in her mouth, the guys moved around taking turns,

Suddenly she was on her and knees, a cock in her mouth. Two rough hands on her hips and a cock head pushing past her pussy lips.

Hands gripping her tits. orgasms rolling over her body. Someone was under her sucking her nipples and breasts. She was spanked.

Cum shot down her throat again, a soft cock now replaced with a new hard on. Then an amazing double, the guy being sucked did not last long and he came in her mouth just as the guy fucking her came in her pussy. She came, she collapsed. She found herself rolled on her back.

Legs pulled apart, and someone larger but not huge was battering her dripping cum filled pussy. A cock pressed against her mouth again but she was cumming too hard to suck. Two other guys were sucking her nipples, roughly squeezing her tits.

The guy fucking her, reached under to grab her ass, and then worked a finger or two into her ass. He came in her. She came.

A break was taken as they let her collect herself. She drank some water, hands gently caressed her legs and back, someone had his arm around her supporting her as she stood at the bar.

Slowly the gentle caressing became sexual, her ass , her breasts, he cum dripping pussy we rubbed, her boss behind her slipped finger in her scooping up cum, then used it to lube her ass then he fingered her.

Each of her nipples were being sucked, she felt her juices and cum running down her legs, fingers stretched her orgasmed tightened pussy, fingers gently worked in and out of her ass.

The fingers pulled away, she felt herself bent forward over a bar stool, something colder and wet was rubbed against her rosebud, her legs spread open, and fingers slid easily inside her, then out, a hand spread her ass cheeks and she felt the familiar head of her bosses cock pushing against her tight opening, sliding in, slowly, letting her relax, not that she needed it at this point.

He pressed all the way into her and grabbed her hips, she gripped the bar to support herself, an anal orgasm building, she heard herself scream "FUCK MY ASS MAKE ME CUM" She heard guys say what a hot slut she was, someone called her a dirty slut, she did not care, she came, her clit was being rubbed, she came harder. Her boss came.

The bar stool spun a bit, she was bent over it, a cock was in her mouth, someone else entered her ass. Neither lasted long, but she had to tell them two was enough back there.

Next she was back on the floor, on the cushion, someone tit fucked her and came on her face, others fucked her and came in her, At least one, pulled out of her pussy and fed her his sloppy cock as she tasted herself, the others who had cum in her and then his cum.

She knows she got DP'd at some point, the rest of the night a blur.

Her boss brought her home to me, he explained what happened, she was too tired to care, a mess. She wore his bathrobe and her sneakers, her clothes in her purse except for her panties which disappeared.

She was too worn out for a bath or shower, so I just put her to bed as is. I noticed cum in her hair, on her face and its, leaking out of her, sex bruises, hand prints on her ass, a few hickies on her tits.

The next morning, I bathed her and showered her, washing her hair, we made love.

I love my slut

# 13. We Ended Up In a Parking Lot

Late night online just looking for someone to have some fun with. I matched with this white woman late 30s around 11pm. It was late but she lived a short drive away. I'm in Manhattan she's in Fort Lee Jersey just across the bridge so it's just a 15min drive. As a joke I told her stores are about to close soon so if she wants me to come over she has to let me know now so I can buy some condoms.

She gives me her address and I jumped in the shower to freshen up then headed to her place. About 5 mins into the drive she messages me again. I'm already about to hit the bridge and she asks if I left the house yet. I told her yes I'm almost to you. She told me her daughter came home and now I couldn't come. I told her that's alright since I'm on my way already we can just meet up and talk or something. She agrees.

I get there and park down the street and see her walking over. She gets to my car and she asks me for my ID. I was real confused but I agreed and pulled it out giving it to her she checks it out then tells me she's texting her friend my name and address for safety. She got in the car and we talked for maybe 20mins before I start reaching over squeezing her thighs. I just decided to pull my dick out for her to see and play with. She turns the flashlight on her phone and starts to inspect my dick.

She then asks if I have a condom. I told her no because we were just supposed to talk. She kept playing with my dick and I put my hand on the back of her head and guided her down to my dick. She sucked my dick for a little while I was about to cum in her mouth but she stopped. She was gonna leave but I asked if I could drive her back to my place since I live close but she didn't want to be gone that long.

I remembered passing a parking lot a block or two away and told her we could go there. I drove to the parking lot and parked in a dark hidden spot. She got her pants off and got on top of me and started to ride me. She told me not to cum inside of her so I would tell her to slow down when I was about to cum. Then we got in the backseat I was standing up outside of the car. I'm tall so it's just better this way lol. I fucked her doggystyle then she sucked my dick again and I shot my load all over the ground.

We both fixed ourselves I drove her back home and went home happy.

# 14. My best friend's mom

When I was 20 I became the unknowing beneficiary of learning that my best friend's mom is a hotwife.

I grew up across the street and two doors down from the Kraus family. I was an only child. They had a daughter two years older than me and a son my age. Their son, Tommy, was like a brother to me. We did everything together growing up. As we got older we did double dates often and then we even went to the same college.

One weekend in the fall of our junior year of college we came home. There was a neighborhood party up the street and I went with Tommy and his girlfriend, Erika. As luck would have it Erika's parents were gone for the weekend, so I knew that she and Tommy would be bugging out early so they could go fuck their brains out. You can't blame a guy when that opportunity comes along. Since I was single at the time I decided to stay and get drunk.

Tommy's parents, Rick and Laura, were also at the party. To say that I had a crush on Laura Kraus would be an understatement. She was/still is the quintessential trophy wife. She is drop dead gorgeous. Her makeup is always done impeccably. She always seems to be dressed to the nines, even when she was "dressed down." My buddies and I always gave Tommy a hard time about how hot his mom was. He would get pissed but he had to see it. We joked about whether or not her blonde hair was natural and how we would love to see her pussy to know for sure.

Well, I was feeling no pain as I was drinking with Tommy's dad, Rick. Laura was moving around, being her normal, flirty self.

Laura was wearing a red wrap-around style blouse with a revealing neckline, tight jeans, and knee high stiletto heeled boots. My parents normally would have been at the party, but they had gone out of town for a family wedding for someone I barely knew. Rick seemed to notice that my eyes kept finding and following his wife. He just grinned and dipped his drink.

As the night got late he pulled Laura aside and chatted with her. Laura then came up to me and grabbed my arm. She said, "You're pretty drunk. Why don't you walk back with us, so we know you are safe." Who was I to disagree with a gorgeous woman who had my arm? I left the party with Laura and Rick, with Laura still holding on to my arm.

As we got to their place I started to separate when Laura suggested I come in to their place for another drink. Hmmmm? More time with a beautiful woman and being drunk? I was down with that. I followed them into their gorgeous house and down to their basement where they have a man cave with a bar, pool table, large screen TV, etc.

Rick grabbed me a bottle of beer, poured Laura a shot, and perched himself on a stool behind the bar with his captain and coke. Laura downed her shot and slammed the glass on the bar and walked over to me. She set my beer on the bar and moved in real close. She asked me, "Jason, so you know what a hotwife is?" I was stunned and silent. Laura explained, "I like to fuck. Rick likes me happy. I get to fuck pretty much whomever I want and Rick likes to watch me fuck when he can. I want to fuck you! I know you've lusted after me for years and now is your time." My eyes were wide open and my jaw dropped in disbelief. Rick nodded, grinned, and motioned to me with a toast and sipped his drink.

Laura pulled me to her and kissed me, thrusting her tongue into my mouth as her one hand grabbed my cock as if stiffened in my jeans. Laura then knelt down and snaked my cock out of the fly of my jeans and shorts, stroking it and commenting to her husband that the rumors about my cock length were true! (I am about 10 inches.) Laura licked her lips and went to work on the head of my cock with her lips and tongue while her one hand teased my balls with the long nails on her hand and the other stroked my length. I heard Rick tell her to deepthroat me and I felt her push her mouth onto me and felt the construction of her throat as she slowly inched more of me into her before she pulled off, gagging, drooling, and panting. She resumed and sucked harder, placing my hand on the back of her head. She pulled my cock further into her throat and pulled off again while gasping. "Fuck my mouth with that beast!" I stroked my dick between her lips, my hand holding her blonde hair to keep her steady as I felt her lips touch the base of my cock. As she pulled off I moaned and began spurting cum all over. She quickly latched on to me and swallowed as much as she could after the firsts blasts hit her cheek and forehead. After she guzzled my load she used her fingers to eat up the errant squirts of jizz, moaning with the delight of a famished diner.

I stood there in amazement as the woman, my best friend's mom, who had launched hundreds of wet dreams for me was swallowing my cum like a whore.

Laura stood up and went to Rick and kissed him before coming back to me. She sat on the edge of the pool table and told me to undress completely. She smiled as she worked on her top, exposing her natural 34B breasts encased in a red, lace bra. She then told me to help take off her boots. I had lost some of my erection but was recovering pretty quickly with this goddess before me. I rubbed my hard cock against her boots and she giggled before exclaiming, "Rick! He is a high heel perv, just like you! I love it!" I reached up her calf and unzipped one boot and slid it off her leg and foot and repeated with the other. I then unbuttoned and unzipped her tight jeans. It took some wiggling to get her out of them and see her matching red thong. I leaned in and pulled Laura's legs apart and licked the front of her panties before pulling them right into her slit and then licking her puffy labia as they splayed open. I grabbed the side of her thong panties and yanked them down and whipped them to the side before literally diving my face into her steamy, hairless snatch. I shoved two fingers deep into her twat as licked and sucked in her clit. I finger fucked her hole until she was moaning that she wanted cock.

I climbed between her legs on the pool table and placed the head of my dick at her pussy lips. She wrapped her legs around me to try to pull me into her. I could feel her nails scratching my sides and my ass as she yearned for me to bury myself into her. I slowly slid the full length of my cock in to the hilt as I heard a guttural sound emit from her as her eyes closed. Laura's hips started rocking in rhythm with me and I felt her hot pussy clench and unclench around my hard member. I leaned in and kissed this wanton beauty deeply as she moaned into my mouth and my dick continued to ravage her slick hole.

Laura spread her legs as wide open as they could go and I propped myself up on my hands so I could thrust as deeply as possible into her hotness before I felt my body start to tense and I shot jet after jet of hot cum deep into her.

I collapsed on top of her, panting. I felt my cock slowly soften and slip from her pussy and felt cum ooze from her hole.

I lifted myself off this gorgeous woman and stood up. I took a drink of my beer and said, "I cannot believe this just happened."

Laura smiled and said, "Believe it, mister. You were fabulous. Your cock is amazing!" Rick added, "I do believe you are going to get to experience more with Laura." She grinned, looked at me and nodded in agreement.

# 15. I didn't choose this!

Well, I didn't start out being a cuck intentionally. I still don't understand why it makes my cock hard!

My story

we were married when I was 22 and she 21. Both just got out of college and I worked in office during the day and she was a nurse working nightshift in a hospital. I thought our marriage was pretty normal with ups and downs. We both from broken homes but dedicated Christians with typical family values. Her father died when she was young which is important as she had Daddy issues that neither of us understood.

After 2 small kids and 15 years of marriage, she sat me down one day and told me she needed to tell me something. This was at a time where we had some pretty serious conversations about marriage, life, etc.... but there was something very grave in her demeanor that day. I couldn't imagine what she was being so serious about but I knew it was going to be bad simply because she never approached me like this. My thoughts turned immediately to a Jerry Springer show and I really wanted to get up and check to make sure Jerry wasn't hiding in the kitchen waiting to surprise me. And, well...... It was almost that bad. She told me, I have a confession to make, I ... I cheated on you ―― WHAT????? When, who, how, WHY???? I'm sorry, I didn't ever want you to know – but I have to tell you because - tears, silence, more tears - because I want us to grow stronger as a team. And then a slowly using few words as possible she admitted "It was a long time ago, I made a mistake, and it has never happened again". Stunned silence............ well, I want to know who and when. Long silence. "I'm not sure that is healthy for you to know." Well FUCK healthy, FUCK you. If you did this, you are going to tell me everything I want to know and you are going to tell me right now. If you don't, I'm NOT leaving the house, but YOU are - and ill pack your crap right now....

loooonng pauses between words. Very hard for her to say. And very hard to hear. She couldn't recall when exactly but just that it had been shortly after she was working at a hospital when we were first married Night shift. She was working in a busy and intense setting with little or no supervision and was at times placed in stressful situations beyond what she was comfortable with.

Little help or advice from anyone, especially the doctors, as they were typically arrogant condescending pricks. However, one of the doctors was always so nice to her. Very professional and always willing to explain and teach things. He never minded her asking questions regardless how basic they were. And he always was at the hospital and even started checking in her to see how she was doing. After a few months, they even had some time to sit and learn about each other's life. They both shared that they were Christians and she was excited to learn that this wonderful doctor was a Christian and was a deacon in a prominent local church. They even had long talks about the Bible and religious views. Now she had looked to him with admiration and appreciation since the moment she met him as a physician. Now she began to look up to him in other ways as well, As a leader, as spiritual advisor. She claims that she did not have sexual attraction to him, but retrospectively, it's easy to see how he was being built up in her mind as a father figure.

Six months or so had passed. One evening, a very sick patient had passed away. Frightening time for medical people because your mind wonders if you missed anything to prevent death. He made his rounds and saw that she was shaken and upset. He stepped to her and told her, there was nothing anyone could do.

You are the best nurse and I always want you on my team! And with that he gave her a hug. A nice long sincerely platonic hug. She apparently cried on his shoulder for a few minutes.

A couple of days later, the doctor was the one under pressure and my wife could see him stressing. He turned to her and said, I could use some hug therapy right now. She answered him with…. a hug. A platonic well intentioned hug. They talked and joked about it and shared with patients how hug therapy can warm the human spirit.

A few weeks later, they were each busy and tending to their duties and they passed each other in the hallway. As they approached each other in the hallway, they slowed their pace and she said the Doc held out his right hand and just asked "Hug Therapy?" She did not verbally reply but reached out with her hand, and as their hands grasped he deftly reached with his other hand to the doorknob behind him which happened to be a one stall unisex bathroom, and he gently tugged her with him into the bathroom and the door automatically closed.
He hugged her tightly and she noticed. It felt so wonderful. He was so strong, so wise, and she felt so secure that he was holding her and that HE, this wonderful doctor, has given her this incredible wonderful support. She said she for once on her life felt like she had a father who loved her and accepted her as she was. She told me that she wasn't sure how the long the hug lasted but it went on for a long time. And then, she noticed something. Something was beginning to poke her in the stomach. Must be a flashlight in his pocket, but, no… Doesn't seem, Could it be?? After a few minutes she knew it was most certainly was, a rock hard erection jutting into her abdomen. And she noticed it was being intentionally held against her abdomen, not being lewd, but most definitely intentionally held so that she would feel his hard cock. But she did not pull away. Something kept her there. And he smartly kissed her on the forehead and said excellent hug therapy and then departed to tend to patients.

She confessed to me that she knew that kind of behavior had gone too far and was inappropriate but she needed the security and reassurance so badly that in her mind she was rationalizing that his body response was just a normal male reaction and that he meant no ill intent towards her. After all, he is a doctor and a Christian.

It was a few weeks later until they worked together again. And just as in the last meeting, they passed in the same spot in the same hallway and he again extended his hand and they slipped quietly into the bathroom. However, this time, as they entered, he deftly flipped off the light switch and their hug quickly developed into a hug of passion. She felt his hands all over and they were kissing not the little friendly kiss on the cheek or forehead but full on tongue swapping. And she recalled his hands were all over her. She said she doesn't recall removing her clothes but somehow she quickly ended up completely naked. His scrub pants were around his ankles and the rock hard erection that was jutting into her abdomen was now throbbing in her hands. She knelt before him and briefly sucked on his cock. But just for a minute as he placed his hands under her arms and lifted her back to her feet. His fingers went to her pussy she moaned and was embarrassed because as his fingers penetrated her pussy made a loud wet squelching sound. Her cunt was literally soaking wet with excitement.

He wasted little time. He gently turned her around so that she could hold onto the handicap bars next to the toilet, and before she knew what was happening she felt his huge erection slide right up inside of her cunt. He was in her solidly and firmly and she said that his cock felt like a big hot iron fire poker. She then told me that all she could think of at that exact moment was ME, and how much she loved me. Wtf .... I told her that doesn't make any sense at all. "I know, I'm so sorry, I should have made him stop".

Really? You Think?

But you didn't stop him did you, Did You? "No…. I'm sorry, I didn't".

I guess now you are gonna tell me you didn't even like it, right ?, didn't even have an orgasm I bet, I'm sure it was just awful for you…. Silence. ….

But since you felt so bad about it, I'm sure it was just a onetime thing, right? ••••, you should have seen the look on her face when I asked that. I asked her how long did it go on…. She said 2 maybe three or four months.

3-4 months? So, that means you saw him 3-5 times a week for 3-4 months and you did it every single time you saw him. ….. Yes ……..

So there it was. My sweet and innocent newly married wife at 21 years of age was bending over a toilet and letting a 40 year old man stick his bare cock and pump her cunt full of his semen. Or better yet, that wholesome clean little church going girl knelt in the floor of a hospital bathroom while a forty year old man rubbed his cock on her face, in her hair, and she licked and sucked on his pecker until he spilled his semen in her mouth.

And she swallows. Always.

So that is where I'll leave the tale.

I obviously embellished this. But I assure u it is 100% true. I asked her lots of questions about it.

I do know:

- he came in her pussy – always without a condom.
- He fucked her from behind – it's the only position she mentioned
- he was 20 years older
- he was circumcised.

I feel sure that in 3-4 months they fucked in about every conceivable position one can get into while fucking in a public bathroom.

She won't tell me if his cock was big.

She also won't tell me how many times it happened.

I know that in future liaisons she would meet him in a bathroom (always in a hospital bathroom) and suck his dick. And they did it in several different bathrooms.
She says they never went out to hotel. Only fucked in bathrooms.

Now curiously enough, I also work in hospitals and I have actually been to a couple of the bathrooms after knowing this just to see where these trysts occurred. That is probably is a little weird. But it was somehow comforting at the time to see the exact location of where this occurred. And stranger yet, as I saw the handicap bars and tried to picture how she might have held onto them and picturing where she stood while being fucked, my cock grew hard. Ashamed and embarrassed inwardly, but still oddly aroused, I pulled out my cock and began masturbating furiously. I quickly shot ropes of semen onto the same floor that my wife knelt on 15 years prior while sucking the old doctor's cock.

One of the bathrooms was in a more public section of the hospital and it was a MENS room. It was not the most sanitary bathroom in the world. And I know that this was the bathroom that on at least one event occurred where she sucked on him. When I entered the bathroom I immediately noting the strong smell of stale musty urine that happens is common in older tile floor bathrooms from the grout becoming saturated with the nauseating ammonia odor of urine. And this is the place where my wife, my beautiful innocent wife either knelt on her knees or sat on the toilet performing fellatio to a forty year old man. Damn. After learning of that incident - I accused her of cheating with others. She did admit to one other affair that occurred just before we actually married. I am not convinced that there are no others.

# 16. Short first crazy time

We were a fairly new couple. I arranged for me and the gf to meet a guy at a wooded area. We got into his vehicle and had some small talk. Then I had the gf lean back into me and I let her tits out of her shirt and started squeezing and playing with them. I was telling him what a slut she was and what she liked done to her. I then had her lay her head on my lap face up and continued to play with her tits and started to pull up her skirt. I finger banged her and played with her pussy while he took pics and made comments. I then put her face down on my lap and she sucked my cock in front of him. The first of many crazy things we've done.

xxxxxxxxxxxxxxxxxxxxxxxxxxxxxxx

When I was a freshman in high school I dated a boy for a short time who was a senior. Sometimes we double dated at the drive in. We spent most of the time making out and petting. Watching and being watched made it more fun. Sometimes when the second movie came on we would switch dates.

xxxxxxxxxxxxxxxxxxxxxxxxxxxxxxxxxx

My sexy young wife at the time agreed to go to a topless beach A Latino guy kept going by and checking her out Finally he came up to us and asked if we had a beer to share with him. He sat with us and chatted telling my 21 year old wife that she was beautiful and she should roll her bikini bottoms up to really show off her sexy hips all the time staring at her big full tits and hard nipples. I realized my young wife loved the attention and that she was an exhibitionist and I was so hard and excited by this he told us that there was a spot up the beach where we could all get completely nude so after a brief talk we decided to try it I got so hard when he removed his swim

Suit exposing a very long thick hard uncut cock to my wife. Her eyes riveted to it he told her to relax and remove her bottoms and I nodded to her that it was ok as I removed mine he then told my wife that her body was so beautifully complimenting her waist m length hair and hard round ass She looked like a young Jennifer Anniston . He then moved very close to her as she lay between us and he gently placed her hand on his big thick cock As he rubbed oil on my wife's 38 dd s I watched as she pumped his big cock in her small hand. His balls bouncing as he fingered my wife he moaned softly and my wife now began to stroke my cock also I was out of my mind with lust and a bit of jealousy because this was brand new to us but I always fantasized About it . My wife Lisa groaned and came on his fingers bucking her hips wildly and this was too much for me I shot a huge load as she pumped my cock and he soon groaned and I watched my wife closely staring as he pumped streams of cum high and onto his belly We put our suits on and he kissed my wife deeply. His tongue going deep into her mouth and asked for our phone number. I wasn't sure about that but this was so incredibly hot that I gave him our number he ended up coming to our home later but that's another story All completely true. In fact this was the start of our wife sharing adventures for many years. She got to feel that huge cock unloading inside her that night and I watched and felt my first sloppy seconds he fucked her twice and then I climbed on. Wow. We were hooked and she was only 21. I was 29

# 17. Wife's Surprising Fantasy

My wife and I are both Asian Americans, she's in her mid 40s and I just turned 50. We are both in great shape still and enjoy an active sex life.

While we were having sex the other day, I asked her what her fantasy was, and she gave her standard reply, which is to have a threesome with 2 guys. She said she wants a cock in her mouth and in her pussy at the same time. This is nothing new, and it's something that we've talked about and fantasized about repeatedly.

I then asked her if she would enjoy it if after the two guys cum in her, she'd enjoy two more guys coming into the room and fucking her. I thought she might be turned off or even grossed out, but she said that she'd love it. This turned me on so much. She said she would really enjoy having a second load in her mouth and a second load in her pussy. Wow, I almost came instantly when she said that.

I asked her if she'd enjoy two more guys after that, so guys number 5 and 6. She said she would not want two more guys to fuck her, but she said that she'd want a guy to eat her out. She said that the idea of a guy eating her cum filled pussy turned her on b/c it means that the guy finds her so sexy that he'd eat another mans cum out of her. I came so hard when she said this!

I then thought about this conversation and jerked off to it a couple of times. So hot! I hope we can make at least some version of this a reality someday.

# 18. My new mature neighbor

I first saw her in July. She was moving into an Apartment down the hall from me. I couldn't help noticing her long well defined legs in a pair of wedge sandals. Wearing a pair of short shorts and pulling it off very nicely for her age. I've never been one to fancy mature women. So I was just being a kind neighbor when I carried a few Boxes into

Her new place. She thanked me and I gave her my name and

Apt number if she needed anything and headed off to my side job at a local bar in NYC

It was there a week later we meet again.

She wanted to thank me again and help her meet new friends.

I was guessing her age at about 55. And very attractive. Low mileage and we'll maintained if you know what I mean.

She explained she just finalized her 2nd divorce. She's a recently retired flight attendant. He caught her cheating. She regrets it for the kids but life goes on. They're Grown and gone.

She was enjoying her Martinis and getting flirty with me. It was about then I started to imagine her naked. And I liked what I was seeing. She stayed to closing time which was earlier than usual. She had me throbbing as she grabbed my hand walking home.

When we got to her door I went to kiss her and she grabbed me by my belt and pulled me into her place as my tongue darted in her warm mouth. Before I knew it we were on her sofa and she was sucking my dick as I untied her halter.

To be honest it wasn't long before she made me cum in her wanting mouth. Whew... she was very understanding. She rolled us a joint and I made us a batch of Kamikazes and we jumped into her king size bed in her air conditioned bedroom and made love for hours.

For 60 years young she kept my 40 yr old dick up all night long. We've tried to hook up once a week since and it gets better every time

# 19. Reminiscing

After partying this weekend my wife was in one horny mood. Saturday night we were lying in bed talking about how we first met and all our sexcapades.

Funny how this one story brought back a ton of memories from how we first got into the fantasy of sharing her.

When I first met her I was staying at my aunt's house, she rented me a room. My cousin, Tim, and I hung out all the time.
I met my Mrs. at the local pub, my cousin fancied her friend.
A couple of weeks dating her, we went to the night club, she had arranged for my cousin to hook up with her friend.
We called it a night early, went back to aunts house, as she was away, we had the house to ourselves.
I was making out with my Mrs., cousin making out with friend. She couldn't get in to him so she called it a night and left. He seemed pretty bummed out she done a runner. Me, him and my Mrs. chatted about how rude of her to do that. We put tunes on, drank a fair bit into the early hours. Taking turns dancing with my Mrs.
Seeing that we had been only dating a few weeks, I had no jealousy or anything.
I have never done this before, never been in this type of situation. Making out with my girlfriend in front of another male.
Tim was sitting in a chair facing me and my Mrs. on the couch.
She was getting frisky with me, grabbing my crotch when she seemed he wasn't looking. She started making out with me. I felt a little uncomfortable knowing my cousin was there with us. I mentioned this to her. Tim said don't bother him. Encourage to continue.

We were kissing side by side. Felt her tits up over her blouse.

I was getting turned on. Don't know if it was playing with her tits or cause of another male in the room that could see.

I pulled her up on my lap. We were making out fiercely; she was grinding on my lap. Slipped my hand in between her legs to feel her warm pussy through her knickers.

I ran my hands around to her ass. Lifting up her denim skirt.

She immediately pushed her skirt back down, continued to make out with me.

I did this a few more times. She kept pushing her skirt back down. I remember this was turning me on big time. Showing my cousin her ass, even though she had knickers on.

She eventually climbed off taking me by the hand to my room.

She said to me when we were in the room why did I keep lifting her skirt up?

All I could say was "just teasing Tim"

the next day Tim did tell me he liked what he had seen.

It hit me at that point. Why would I do this to someone I'm dating, she is mine and only mine was my thought back then.

From that point I was the stupid jealous type husband. I hated it when another guy would chat her up or even say something in the wrong way to her.

Eventually I got my own flat, she moved in with me at this time. We had been dating about 8 months by then.

We were young, horny all the time. Sex was nonstop, almost daily. Hard to believe that now lol but is true.

One evening we were lying in bed, foreplay, usually pillow talk when she asked what was one of my fantasies.

I didn't have to think twice, I said "me, you and another woman". The average male fantasy.

She replied something like "typical"

I asked what hers was. Half expecting for her to say her and 2 guys.

But she said, "to be caught or watched having sex"

this intrigued me by her fantasy, asking her to explain.
Her very first story she had ever told me was about her and me, on a secluded beach, having sex. A couple of men out in a boat who could see us, watching us have sex.

Listening to her tell me this blew my mind. That is so exciting I thought, I told her I do like that scenario.
When ever we had sex I would always have her tell me a story during foreplay.
they progressed with each time she told this story, from the men watching us, the men rowing closer to us, to them coming ashore jerking off as they watched us.
She did not mention about them joining us...
one evening I had to stop her during the story telling, I asked what would she do if they wanted to join in.
she said she couldnt allow that, i asked her why?
She said "because that would upset you"
I told her we have gone this far, they have seen you naked having sex, so whats the difference if they touched you? Besides its just story telling...

this opened up a whole new side to our love making.
When she started to have them interact with us, it turned me on big time.
Listening to her tells me what they are doing to her, what she is doing to them...always made me shoot my load...

one time I asked her if there is a face to these men? Do we know them?
The very first time I asked that she said no one in particular. But the following times she started to add names to who they were.

The very first name she used was Tim, my cousin.
I stopped her in her story telling, why Tim? Do you fancy him?
Would you like for him to actually join you?
Her reply was "he has seen my ass, so why not"
so that evening had stuck in her head all that time. But she had

never mentioned it to me. But I know why, it was the being watched fantasy of hers....

I said to her "I want to hear what could have happened that evening then?"
she never hesitated to start the story off.
her sitting on my lap, us making out, me lifting her skirt, how it actually happened, then she added the new fantasy part....
she said I unbuttoned her blouse, taking it off, unclasping her bra, throwing it at Tim.
Her back still to him, me sucking on her nipples.
She turns back to see Tim now has his cock out, wanking off.
she proceeded saying I pulled her knickers off, Tim watching every moment, her lifting her ass up so he can see what was going on...

I nearly shot my load listening to her tell me this, I had to stop her playing with my cock..
Oh you like that do ya? she said
carried on with the story,
she climbed off of me, turned around, straddled me showing Tim her fully pussy and tits, watching him jerk off to us...
you like that she asked me
hell ya......
she motioned for Tim to stand us, pulling him in to kiss her.
Tim starts to fondle her tits as they kiss. Then Tim runs his hand down to rub her clit as I'm pumping her.
By this time in her story she came hard as I was rubbing her clit.
Oh you like that to I said to her...
she just carried on with the story.
She leaned back in to me, our faces met, we started to kiss, me still inside her, she hand guiding Tims cock to her pussy.
Guiding him in to her, taking us both.....

That was enough for me; I flew on top of her listening to this wild fantasy of hers. Needless to say I came quickly.

From that night on all I kept thinking about was to see her getting fucked by another man....
I knew it was just a fantasy, how would I really react? Would I be jealous? Would she actually do this? It was eating at me for the longest time as we had discussed these were just pillow talk fantasies that were it....nothing else...

It was many years after that time in our marriage when the stories started to actually fulfilling a fantasy.
During those years, I encouraged her to flirt with a select few of our friends we used to hang around with. We discussed about how could we ever ask a friend to join us, what would their reactions be? What would they think of us? Would that ruin a friendship? The list was never ending.
One year, one of our neighbours who used to come over some evenings or weekends to have beers with us. This one night he said to us he is taking a massage course, something he always wanted to do he said.
We didn't get into any discussion about his massage course until a month or so afterwards.
He came over the one weekend; I asked how's his course going?
He said he likes it, just wished he could get more practice.
When he left I mentioned to my wife that I think he was offering his services. She sort of laughed telling me she had the same feeling.
So I asked if she wanted a massage from him, it could lead to one of our fantasies.
She didn't say yes nor did she say no. it was a "thinking" response. Shrugged her shoulders.
I brought it up again with her one evening, while in bed asking her would she be naked for a massage.
She told me that she always keeps her panties on at the spa. But has never had a male massage her there.
After thinking about it she told me, that she is not really attracted to our neighbor, so don't think I would like to have him give me a massage.

That was her feeling so I had to respect them.

We still had our "pillow chats" but not as frequent as they used to be.
It was a week or so coming up to my birthday.
We were sitting at the bar after a meal, having a few drinks. She seemed a little less chatty than normal.
Then out of the blue, it hit me like a ton of bricks by what she had said to me.
I know what you would like for your birthday. She said.
I had no clue as to what she was going to say. What's that then? Another sweater? Lol I replied.
She said "a 3some"
I nearly fell off the chair when those words came out her mouth.
I asked "are you serious?"
she said to me "yes, that's if you would like that?"
I honestly didn't know what to say. All I thought about was she winding me up? Teasing me? Is she having an affair? Wtf my mind was reeling.
So I asked her did she have someone in mind? Have you asked them?
She said she has someone in mind and no haven't asked them yet.
I did ask her how in the world are you going to bring this conversation up with them? How do you know they would be into it?
All she told me was "I know, don't worry"
we called it a night then, as soon as we got home I asked her was it one of our friends?
She said "no"

around this time we had dabbled playing on the internet chat rooms. Wife had flashed a few guys who she chatted with. She enjoyed getting them off. For me the excitement was her talking dirty to these men and her watching them jerk off and for her to show them her tits on cam. Always led to get sex afterwards.

But thinking about actually doing this in real life was all new to us. How would I react? How would she react? Again a thousand thoughts threw my mind.

So we sat on the couch, started to discuss who this other guy is. She had been at her new job as a manager for about 6 months. One of the other managers, Morgan, had been having lunch with my wife for a month or so now. She told me he wanted a sympathetic ear to chat to about his life.

He girlfriend he had been with for around 8 yrs stopped having sex with him a year back. She left him around that time.

He told my wife at lunch one day could she hook him up with one of her friends.

She said she could do that. Their daily chats were always about him not having a relationship and hasn't had sex in over a year.

My wife told me that he is a handsome guy, pretty much fit, just very shy and quiet around the ladies at work. But for some reason he felt comfortable talking to her.

I said maybe it's because you are about 10 yrs older, a mother figure lol

that didn't go down to well. Lol

so I asked her what made you think about him joining us in a 3some?

She said that the day or so before he told her "I going to hire a hooker, I need sex badly"

my wife told him that's a bad choice, you don't know what and who you are getting."

he said he doesn't care.

So she said I told him "I will think about one of my friends to hook you up with"

his response to my wife was "I just wished you weren't married" she told me she seemed complimented by his choice of words.

We came to the decision she was going to ask him the next day at work. We went to bad, had sex but nothing mentioned about the 3some.

The next day I would never forget how I felt, nervous, anxious, maybe scared...

when she got home she didnt get into a conversation right away.
While we were cooking dinner I had to ask her.
Did you speak to Morgan?
She said "yes I did"
well? What did he say, what did you say? I asked
she told me how the conversation went.
At lunch he asked her if she spoke to one of her friends? She told
him no as she couldn't think of a good match for him. Anyways
most of our friends are married.
But I have another option she told him
he asked her what was that?

Now I couldn't believe I was hearing this from my wife, never in
a million years would I ever hear her say this.

She said I just came out with it to him, asked him if he would be
interested in joining us for a 3 some.
His initial response was "no I couldn't do that."
she asked him why not?
He told her he is straight, wouldn't like to be in a predicament
where another male would touch him.
She laughed telling me this what she said to him.
She said "there will not be any of that, my husband is as straight
as an arrow, he not into that at all"
she said his tone changed after that.
He asked her whose idea was this. Was it hers, was it mine?
so she told him it was both our ideas, we have been married a
long time, we love each other very much, if my husband was on
board then I wouldn't entertain this at all she told him.
Of course he had doubts too. Asking her what I was like, do I get
jealous or angry?
She told him we have been discussing this type of sexual behavior for many years, it's just fantasies, nothing else.
He didn't say yes to her at lunch she told me she said he wants to
meet you. So we going out tomorrow night for a few drinks with
him, for him and I to get to know one another.

I still couldn't believe this was happening, sort of a daze thinking about it. Is my wife willing to give up her pussy to another guy? How would she feel when it comes to her getting undressed, him seeing her naked?

The scenario has been running through my mind for years but now it could be reality, how would I feel? It far different then her exposing herself on cam or listening to her tell stories.

We met Morgan at the pub around 7ish, he seemed like a polite guy, stood up to shake my hand greeting me.

We hit it off, talking about sports, his work my work etc...

A few hours in the meet and greet with him he said to me I hear you have a birthday coming up. I told him ya, tomorrow.

Not once did he mention about his chats with my wife nor the offer she put out to him.

I had to say something, thinking now about it, it was the alcohol courage. Otherwise I couldn't bring this conversation up.

I said to him "I heard that my wife has given you an offer, sort of a birthday present for me?"

he didn't really look me in the eyes, he nodded yes, asked me what was my thoughts about it?

I told him about my wife and I have been having these fantasy discussions for many years. Never really pursued them as we were nervous about doing it.

He wanted reassurance I assumed.

He asked me if I would be comfortable kissing my wife, seeing her naked, touching her.

Listening to him say this started to get me horny, never heard another man talk about my wife like this.

I told him I would love to see all that happen.

We chatted a little about it. It was getting late. We didn't want to rush into this either, especially when we had been drinking.

We called it a night; my wife gave him a kiss on the lips. My wife always kissed other men on the cheek. Never seen her kiss another man on the lips.

At that point something hit me... I wasn't getting 2nd thoughts; it was about my wife kissing another man.

When we got home she asked me what I thought about him.

I told her "he's very polite and seems like a stable guy"

she asked if I still would like to go through with this?

I told her of course as long as she is too, not just doing this to fulfill my fantasy.

She said yes she would like to try it...

as we were lying in bed, we talked about it some more. The only thing that I could think of I told her was the kissing. In my mind kissing is for love between the 2 people.

She disagreed, she told me "you know I love to kiss during sex, it turns me on"

I explained the "love/kissing" thoughts I had. She said to me "I disagree, its part of love making, nothing else." then she said if you feel that way then we should do it.

I actually felt really comfortable by what she said.

I asked her if there's something that she wouldn't like to do? Now this blew my mind.

she yes "yes, only I can go down on her" "you are the only guy whose has ever gone down on me, I don't want anyone else doing that"

my reply was "that one thing I would like to see happen," "the thought of seeing a guy licking you down there, tasting you."

but she said "no I don't think so"

so I respected her wish telling her I would only go down on her before his cums in her"

she found that funny. I didn't lol

so we came to the conclusion this was going to happen tomorrow night, that's if Morgan was still on board. She said to me I may have frightened him.

The next day I had the feelings again, this time I felt a little jealous. Thinking, "what if they having sex now? Without me?"

my wife and I have mentioned this before, she would never do that to me, nor would I to her. So I blew that thought out of my head.

When she got home she said we going for a meal, not to cook dinner.
We meeting Morgan at the restaurant for 6ish,
so it's a go then? I asked
just get ready and clean up she told me as she went off to have a shower.
While she had her shower I took a bath, thinking about how the night is going to go, will it really happen? I had to stop myself from jerking off.
I got out, went to our bedroom, my wife was sitting on the toilet shaving her legs and pussy.
I had to have a look. Rubbing her pussy, it was silky smooth. Nice...
she already had her clothes out on the bed, a blouse, pencil skirt and her favorite undergarments.
We got dressed, now the nerves were hitting me. Like when you first meet a girl for a date, the butterflies were fluttering big time.
As we drove to the restaurant, we discussed how we think it should go after the dinner. At one point she said to me if there's anything that bothers me during this I have to let her know, it would stop then and there.
I told her I can't imagine any thoughts I would have except me coming to soon. She laughed at that, telling me I better not. I had to control myself.
I would try...can't promise anything.

To say the truth I still had a little doubt about seeing her passionately kissing him. I do know how she likes to kiss. French kissing and all.
But I put that out of my head, I had to.

The meal went smoothly; we had one alcoholic drink each. We never talked about later that evening, just chatted and ate.
Around 8ish we said lets go. Morgan said he will see us at our house. He has to go home first.

During our drive home I said to my wife I think he chicken out.
He won't show.
We got in, opened a bottle of wine. Put some music on, sat on
the couch.
Sure enough the door bell went. Wife got up to answer; I remember to this day that feeling. This is going to happen. My wife is
going to get naked in front of another guy and let him fuck her...
I got him a glass of wine; we sat on the couch, wife in the middle.
To be honest, we must have looked like the wallflowers at the
high school dance. Too nervous to talk.
Had to have been 15-20 minutes when my wife stood, up. all she
said was "fuck this, I guess I have to get this party started."
she stood in front of me, unbuckled my belt, unzipped my trousers freeing my cock, she held on to me as she turned her attention to Morgan, unzipping his pants, pulling his cock out. She
was beating us both off, very badly I would admit, no rhythm at
all. Then again this was the first time pulling on 2 cocks.
I led back watching her beating his cock; Morgan led back
watching her jerking him off.
She let go of us, lifted up her blouse, as soon as her hands went
behind her back to unclasp bra.
I thought I was going to cum.
she let her bra fall to the floor, before I could react; Morgan
leaned forward, cupped her tit and started to suck on her nipples.
I was dazed is all I could say. Seeing this happening right in front
of me, my wife having another man touch her tits.she was staring at me the whole time. She pulled my head into her other tit.
Morgan and I both suck on her nipples. Trying not to touch one
another's head loll
I reach down to put my hand up her skirt. She stopped me. She
stood up, unzipped the back of her skirt, letting it fall to the
floor.
She was standing not a foot from our faces, I was waiting for her
to drop her panties, and she just took both of us by the hands,
leading us to the bed room.

As we both stood next to the bed, she pushed us both back on the bed. The first words out of her mouth was "I could get used to this"
she had never been the dominate one at all.
As we both led on the bed, our boners at 12 o'clock, she proceeded to jerk Morgan and blow me; I had to stop her, pushing her head towards Morgan.
Watching again sliding her lips over his head, down his shaft, I had to stop her from jerking me off. I was at my limit...
I sat up, she was kneeling between his legs, I reached down to take her panties off, I was expecting for her to stand up to allow me to remove them. As I pushed the sides down, the side of her panties ripped. She stopped, looked at me,
"these were my favorite pair. Way to go."
she stood up. Letting her panties fall to the floor. Morgan had his head raised, looking at her smooth silky pussy. I ran my hand up between her thighs, rubbing my finger over her clit.
I said to her that she must be really horny, it's dripping wet.
She led on the bed next to Morgan. He immediately started to massage her tits, their lips locked on to one another's, I stood there looking at them, she turned her head towards me, pointed to her pussy.
She rolled on her back a little, parting her legs. I knew what she wanted, as soon as my tongue hit her clit she shuddered, I sucked on her clit to have her cum her first orgasm.
I was looking up at them, she was on her back. Morgan sucking her one tit, playing with the other.
She reached down, pushed my head away, told me to fuck her, she wanted cock inside her.
I raised her feet up on the bed, parted her legs. As soon as I entered her, watching them kissing, Morgan playing with her nipples. Was enough I could take. I pumped her hard as I came.
She pulled away from Morgan, looked at me, said "really?"lol
I reassured her I won't be a problem. As I led on the bed next to her. She pushed Morgan up, I was kissing her then I felt her rocking up and down, the thought of Morgan in her pussy was driv-

ing me nuts again. I raised my head to look down; she put her hand on my face pulling me back to hers.

I wasn't having any of this; I wanted to see his cock in her. As soon as I looked down, I shot my head back to my wife. What the fuck I mouthed to her. She grinned and shrugged her shoulders, he didn't have his cock in her, and he was licking her pussy like crazy.

1st thing that ran through my mind was "does he know I came?" lol

she came hard against his face. I was rock hard again.

She climbed up on all fours on the bad. Her ass facing Morgan. She guided me up the bed so she could blow me. I was staring down at Morgan pumping my wife from behind. He was constantly looking down at her ass. The visions running through my mind was overwhelming. He is staring at his cock pumping her pussy, he is staring at her arsehole...

again I came as she was blowing me.

It is very rare she gives me a blowjob, only once has she allowed me to cum in her mouth. She must have been really horny that night as she licked me clean.

She rested her head on my stomach, enjoying this new cock inside her. She reached back, held on to his hips. "Cum inside me" she said to him

the only time I've ever heard her say those words was when we first started dating.

Be banged her for a minute or so after her saying that. He pulled out, she rolled on her back. Pulled him on her. She held my hand as they started to kiss.

Between kissing and Morgan going down sucking her nipples, he must have gotten hard again.

Her legs were raised high, Morgan's ass started to thrust back and forth.

I need to see this. I pulled her one leg to the side. Looking at his cock sliding in and out of her pussy. I moved my hand down her tummy; she stopped me before I could touch her clit.

I found out afterwards why that was. She didn't want me to accidentally touch his cock. Fair play I thought.

We had to have been going for about an hour.

When ever wife and I got for an hour she complains her pussy is sore.

When we were done, Morgan started to get dressed, my wife got up to grab her clothes, I led on the bed.

He turned to me, said his goodnights and left the room.

About 10 minutes after I heard the front door close.

As soon as my wife came back in our bedroom, she jumped on me and said "I want you to fuck me now"

I said I could try, but lucky enough I did get hard again.

The next day my wife and I talked about this for ages. Asking one another how we felt.

Actually I was amazed that we both enjoyed the encounter, that I wasn't jealous. My wife really went through with this.

One thing she said was "there was one thing she would have really liked to try"

I asked what that was.

She said DP

I told her I don't think Morgan would have enjoyed that.

She said she would find out.

So we set up another date with Morgan the following weekend.

One thing I said to her that I regretted not doing was take pictures. She stopped me right there. No way in hell would she allow that, bummer I thought?

# 20. Weekend getaway

My wife Duane and I went on a weekend getaway few years back. We rented a small cabin up in north Georgia. The cabin was very nice I had one large bedroom a game room upstairs that had a ping-pong table and a pool table that over at a balcony over the living room. The first day we were there we enjoyed hiking on the boulders up in the mountains just enjoying being with each other. Later that we went to a nice restaurant and ate supper then back to the cabin.

Once back at the cabin Dean went and changed to a very sexy nighty which got me very hard just looking at her. Well it wasn't long before she had my cock out sucking on it. She was given me one of the best blowjobs that she had given in a long time. Next thing I know we are fucking like rabbits on the couch. After we get done we clean up then we go upstairs to the game room.

Once in the game room we play a few games of ping-pong then we move over to the pool table and start playing pool. It was hard to stay focused on the game because every time she been over to take a shot her ass was in my face. So the next time she been over to take a shot I slid my cock in her pussy. It wasn't long before she was sitting on the edge of the pool table and me down on my knees licking her pussy. She came so hard is she squirted all over my face. I sat on the edge of the pool table so she could suck my cock.

After we finish up in the game room we went to bed and fucked one more time before I went to sleep. The next morning when we woke up we fucked one more time then we took a shower together and got all cleaned up. We got dressed and went out and got something to eat and spent the day enjoying the sights shopping just acting like teenagers. On our way back to the cabin we stopped and grab some takeout to eat once we got back to the cabin.

Once we ate we went out on the back deck and enjoy the view and then after the sunset we went to bed to watch TV. Once in bed my hard cock got the best of me and we started fooling around again. I pulled her panties off and wait between her legs started eating her pussy, I would tease it with my tongue I would lick her clit then suck on it until she begged me to stop. We fucked on and off all night long.

The next afternoon when we woke up it was raining so I told Dean that I would jump in the shower and run pick us something up to eat. When I return from the store to my surprise Dean was spread eagle on the kitchen table saying breakfast is served so I did what any man would do set the food down and dive in and start eating pussy. I think that was the best breakfast I've ever had. After I had made her cum we ate our breakfast and went back and got in bed. We fucked on and off the rest of the day while it was raining.

I think we fucked more that weekend then we did on our honeymoon and we are trying to set up another weekend getaway for our 40th wedding anniversary. They probably won't be as much fucking this go on because of our age but there will be fucking going on.

Try not to hammer me too hard because I'm not the best writer in the world. But it was great remembering that weekend.

# 21. The deer camp adventure

We have a camp in greenbrier county. Nothing fancy, open first floor living space and a loft for common sleeping area. Beds are actually several full size mattresses on 2x4 platforms on the floor and a camp chair by each bed.There is no privacy

As you can probably tell by my screen name I am a shared wife, a very happy shared wife. Usually with friends we have know for years. It's not something we do every weekend, or what one would call a lifestyle . Just something we do when the mood hits and the chemistry is right, Seldom do we make specific plans and let thing happen. I said seldom not always. The deer camp was an exception.

This past summer (2015) had been very hectic with no chance of socializing with our friends let alone much quality one on one time with my husband. My husband suggested that we should maybe plan a party or something more intimate. I was more than willing and told him to take care of the details as I was up for anything.

A few days later he told me he had a plan in the works but that I had to agree ahead of time that I would assume a somewhat sub-missive role and be available for whatever came up. When I ask what he had planed all he said was remember college. I got ner-vous scared wet and Horney all at the same time but as always agreed.
Nothing more was said about it.

My husband and four of his buddies always take week off for deer season and head to the mountains to hunt. It's a guy thing in these parts. The week before leaving I would usually start complaint about being left alone. Again that's what wife's do in these parts during deer season. He told me that I should not complain because this year I was going with them as chief cook and bed warmer. I started to make a feeble protest but Mark reminded me of the agreement. I was already wet thinking of the possibly's.

In the past I had sex with two of the four guys (John and Mike) going but not together and too my knowledge one did not know about the other. The other two had no idea about our other life. This was going to be fun or a train wreck and told Mark so but I was still going along for the ride.

We were to pick up John Monday morning. Tom and Eric would be riding with Mike but would not be leaving till later in the day.

When it came time to leave we stopped by to pick up John. Both John and his wife were surprised to see me sitting in the truck. Seems Mark did not tell any one that I was going along on the hunt. Mark explained that Gail would be joining us this week to help out around the cabin so we could hunt more? John was all smiles and his wife told Gail she better get ALL the details when they get back. I should say that John and Beth are both people that we have had sex with before.

The trip up was more or less uneventful. We stopped for breakfast and supplies along the way. There was some minor grouping and joking about how we were going to keep our secret from the others. Mark never said a thing just smiled and drove.

We got to the cabin around 1 and carried in a weeks worth of food and supplies for 6. The only heat or cooking source is wood. Mark was going to pick up a truck load of split wood from a local guy. John offered to stay and help get the cabin squared away. Mark just smiled and said have fun.

There was a lot of talking and playing going on by we did get the

supplies put away. We were done but Mark had not made it back yet. John had ask what else needs to be done and what were the plans for the weekend. I told him I did not know what the plans were only that I was to take care of what ever needed taking care of. John ask if that included his dick. A few minutes later Mark came back to see me bent over the table getting fucked by John. Mark just said hurry up there is fire wood to unload.
So far the week was off to a good start.

My pants back on fire wood unloaded fixing some dinner and waiting on the Others. Mark ask if everything was ok and was I still willing ,I said yes. John was a bit confused But said he was in as long as he got to finish the fuck he interrupted .The rest of the guys showed up while we were eating. They were surprised that I was there. They got their gear stored in the loft. I went about cleaning up after dinner whiles the guys were having a beer on the porch and explaining about my role there. A role I was not even 100% sure of.

Every one came in and sat at the table . Mark said Eric had a question for me. He wanted to know if I had agreed to everything Mark had talked about. I still did not know what it was but my answers was I'm here aren't I. I guess that was good enough. Then Mark began to explain the rules for the week.
I was to be a sex servant.
Each of them showed a piece of paper with a day of the week on it.Mark explained that I would spend one night in each of their beds even thou all the beds were in the same room.
From 9pm to 9am i was private property I belonged to that person to do as he pleased. I was owned but not shared with the other during that time.
From 9am till 9pm I was to be public property. Anyone could use me anyway any place they wanted. It could be one on one or all on one. What ever they wanted. I was not allowed to refuse a request.
John pointed out that it was only 830 kissed me set me on the

couch and stuffed his dick in my mouth. I sucked and licked. He held my head and fucked my face and unload in my mouth.

Mark and Mike watched with a smile Eric was dazed and Tom said it's 9 and I have Monday took me upstairs.

Yes it was going to be a good hunting trip.
NOTE:
There have been several request to know how things went the rest of the week and some emails critical of the events.

For the positive comments and email thank you to the others don't read it. To answer a couple of question. Yes the events with Deer Camp and College Days are true. No I am not a man posting as a women. Yes my husband is on here and he does post under his screen name ( not mine) from time to time but for the most part I post my own pictures and articles . You can be assured If the screen name is WVshared it is me a female of 60 years. Shared for over 40 years.

MONDAY, Because some requested more of the story.

Tom drew Monday night and as 9 hit he took me by the hand and up to the sleeping loft. Latter to be ever known as the fucking loft. Seems Tom had gotten a few down the blouse glimpse of cleavage at a couple of neighbor functions and had been wondering how he could see more. Guess he found out. As anxious as he was he was regardless of what he heard and saw just a few minutes earlier he was still a bit unsure once we got to the loft. I had to reassure him that all was good and I was private property until reverted to community property in the morning. What ever he wanted was his for the taking. You could still hear the others talking below. Tom told me to undress for him. I took off my blouse and was looking for a place to put it when he said throw it over the railing. I did as I was told to the cheers of those below. Next went the pants soon followed by bra and panties to the guys below. This entire time Tom just set and watched. Once naked he had me lay on the mattress he said his wife was a real prude when it came to being naked or sex. He ask if I would play with myself and let him watch. I said yes but had to reassure him of anything he wanted was for his taking he did not have to ask. I spread my legs so he could have a good view then started playing with my pussy. I get real wet when turned on and I was already soaked as my fingers slid in. I closed my eyes and lost myself in my own pleasure not really paying attention to Tom or what he was doing. When I opened my eyes Tom was standing beside me pants around his ankles jerking off. Before I could offer to help he blew all over my stomach and tits. When he saw me rub his cum into my tits and continue to play with my pussy he started to realize I was his. He kicked his pants off and stuck his limp dick in my mouth and told me to clean it up and not stop till it was hard again. As I sucked his dick I continued to play with my pussy and had my first cum of the trip. It was not long before Tom was hard again. He finished undressing and got on the bed between my legs and started licking my pussy. I had to laugh to myself. Tom made the comment he was glad he goy Monday so he could taste my pussy before anyone else got in there. I did not have the heart to tell him Johns dick had already been there and that he was doing a little clean up. He either did not notice or not care. After a few minutes of licking we were both ready for some serious fucking. Tom is not the biggest dick I have had nor the smallest. Being his second go around he had some serious staying power. He started out slow but did not take him long to get into some fast pounding and I came again. He pulled out and rolled me over grabbed my hips and slammed back into me and continued the pounding. After a good hour of some serious sex we went yo sleep. John woke me up two more time. The first time he realized that the others were in the same room sleeping and he was a little shy it was a slow Gentoo fuck under the covers. By that third time he did not care. He pulled me up on all fours and just took me. Doric not care who saw or heard what was going on.

The others were getting dressed for the morning hunt. Tom said he still had two hours of ownership and would catch up later. We showered together and he got a blowjob before 9AM.

Dressed and left to join the rest of the hunters.

Figuring the guys would be back around 1 I took a nap then got dressed and fixed a pot of Chile and relaxed. Last night was enjoyable. And could only wonder what the day was going to bring. And who drew Tuesday.

# 22. Hot Hispanic in the Desert

After spending 20 years in law enforcement, I retired and went into sales, servicing the western United States and mostly California.

I get tons of messages and meet with clients as well as friends when time permits. I'd been chatting with a beautiful Hispanic Milf of social media and was in the low desert of California near Palm Springs and their numerous Casinos.

It was the typical Starbucks meet and greets to see if we were compatible. I told her when I saw her I would give her a big hug and kiss. Her reply was, "Oh really." I wasn't sure if that was a good thing or a bad thing.

I drove up and saw her sitting in her very expensive sports car. I jumped inside and true to my word planted a big kiss on her. Our lips met and it was liked they've known each other for years. My hands began to caress for soft taunt skin. She spends about 5 days a week in the gym. She is extremely petite at 4' 10", brown hair, huge 36 DD implants, with very firm very big dark nipples, and a smooth shaved pussy.

After a nice little make out session we decided to at least grab some ice tea. We kept staring at each other as we talked. We got our tea to go. We made out again, and realized there was too much daylight traffic. I drove to a parking structure and we talked a while until I reached over and kissed her again.

This time my hands grabbed at her big breasts. I found her hard nipples waiting for me. She pulled my head into her as I sucked both of them into my mouth. My hands slipped lower into her jumper and I rubbed her wet pussy over the top of her thong. Once my fingers found their way inside her she let out a moan in my ear. It encouraged me to drive my finger deeper in her, and that's when I felt it..

Her pussy began to pulsate and her whole cervix felt like it was racing to the front for more attention.

I quickly got in the back seat of my big truck and invited her back. No one was the wiser there on the third floor behind tinted windows. I pulled her jumper aside and my mouth found her shaven pussy lips. She tasted so good. She grabbed the back of my head and her hips moved with my mouth.

I reached up and pinched her nipples while I stuck a finger in her and pumped away. She grabbed hold of my head harder and her moaning increased and in about a minute her pussy let go and she squirted a nice shot in my direction. She was a little embarrassed until she found out it turned me on. I reached up and kissed her and she grabbed my face to kiss me back. I went down on her again, and she came a second time squirting even harder. I leaned back opened my pants and let my cock spring free. She had me harder than I'd been for the longest time. Her mouth worked the long shaft up and down before it disappeared down her throat. She was amazing at giving head. Her hands so skilled at stroking the shaft and sucking the head just the way I like it.

I couldn't stand anymore I needed inside her hot pussy. I laid her back on the seat, pulled the jumper aside again and buried myself deep inside her. She was a little taken aback by my size, but soon adjusted. You know that feeling when your cock is gliding in and out so nice, and those panties are rubbing one side of your cock? It was driving both of us wild, although it was a little annoying.

She jumped up, took off the jumper, and I faced forward, watching her bury herself on my throbbing dick. She held the front of the head rest while she rode me reverse cowgirl. I reached up and grabbed her huge breasts. Her body shuddered and she had another orgasm. I ditched my shorts and laid her back of the seat. This time I put my body on her, and began to kiss her as I fucked her tight pussy. Over and over again for the next 15 minutes I could feel her pussy gush juice all over. What a turn on!

Her pussy was so wet, so tight, so yummy. I sucked her clit into my mouth an gave her one more very big, very wet orgasm.

She then came to my cock and began to suck the head while I stroked the shaft. Not going to sugar coat it. I'm 51 year old and this little 49 year old hottie rocked my world. I stroked it until she took over and I told her I was going to explode.

She put her mouth on the head of my cock and sucked the huge load of me as I came. When I was done she moved back. When the second wave started she eagerly planted he lips on my cock again. This happened three more times, and I was drained. We laid there laughing and holding each other.

Surprisingly she turned me on so much that my cock was ready to go like a teenager and I slide it back into her doggie style. She felt so amazing. My cock slowly slid into her and I hold her hips so nice. Her beautiful petite muscular body entranced me.

I saw the flashing lights of the security truck heading our way and I pulled out and we quickly threw on our clothes. Her jumper was soaked! We laughed as we jumped in the front seat and I drove off just before the guy started approaching the truck. Always fun to act like teenagers, even better to cum all over the place.

As I was cleaning out the car later, I had to smile when I felt the huge wet spot on the back seat. Can't wait to visit the desert again!

# 23. Getting My Hotwife

My hotwife enjoyed playing on her own with certain guys. I enjoyed hearing the stories about the fun she had but felt a bit left out. I also had the feeling there were a lot of details I wasn't hearing about which led to this special event.

There was one guy, KJ, my wife only played with alone. They would meet up at hotels, his place or at his office. They mostly chatted through email which I was reading one day as my wife left her email account open on our computer in our home office. The email he had was his first name with a couple of digits at yahoo.com. Pretty easy to replicate. So I created a similar email with one extra digit and decided to email her. Right away she thought I was him. She started talking about some of the recent sex they had and I was getting really turned on.

After a few emails I suggested we go to a hotel that day. I told her that the room would be left ajar and to come in get naked put a blindfold on and be ready. To my surprise she agreed without hesitation

So I'm at the hotel watching her park hoping this continues to go as planned. In a few minutes I walk back into the room and there she is. Naked on her back and blindfolded. I was rock hard. I headed to the side of the bed and guided her head to my cock which she eagerly sucked as I fingered her soaked box. I had my way with her cumming twice. Once in her ass and the second time down her throat. Two things she never let me do before.

It was probably the best sex I ever had with her. I left her there and put some money on the dresser for her as he liked to do. I went home and waited. About an hour later she walks in. I asked how her day was and she said fine. Anything fun happen I asked. She said no nothing special. It took a few hours then I told her what happened. She didn't believe me at first but then realized she's been duped.

Although the sex was hot it bothered me she was doing things with others she wouldn't do with me and having sex without letting me know. She and I had a different view of what the hot-wife was suppose to be.

# 24. First BBC 2

She went to the bed like I told her, she said a couple outside got a good look at her in the window, asked if they were her surprise I told her not this time. I began by tying her hand above the bed, placed the blindfold began twisting her nipples she loves that. She asked again who her present was. I told her it was someone I met on line who wanted to have the experience of an older woman...she asked how old was he I told he 30 all she did was go mmmmmm. I told her he had seen her pics and was in full lust. and almost on cue there was a knock on the door. When opening the door Karen was on full display.

I told him to make himself comfortable that Karen was there for our pleasure. We both got undressed, I had seen pics of his cock but seeing it live he was hard and bigger than me but not huge but the girth I knew will fill Karen mouth or pussy.

He walked to Karen grabbed her boob my the nipple and she moaned, he called her a slut and she said yes she was. He put his cock on her lips and she could barley open her mouth enough. She tried to suck but choked on him. She guessed right away that her toy was her first bbc, she asked that her hands be untied so she could really enjoy him .He untied one hand to start and it went right away to his cock all she said was I was the best hubby, and she was going to enjoy her toy....and she sure did only hole he didn't use was her ass it would never have fit lol

# 25. Sexy topless beach adventure

My sexy young wife at the time agreed to go to a topless beach with me. After a little prodding she removed her top exposing her big dd tits and very hard nipples. I got so hard watching the voyeur guys walking by our blanket and really checking her out. My wife seemed a little embarrassed but very excited to show off for all the guys checking her out. I got so hard that I had to lay on my stomach to hide my rock hard cock bulging in my swim-suit. A Latino guy kept going by and checking her out finally he came up to us and asked if we had a beer to share with him. He sat with us and chatted telling my 21 year old wife that she was beautiful and she should roll her bikini bottoms up to really show off her sexy hips all the time staring at her big full tits and hard nipples. I realized my young wife loved the attention and that she was an exhibitionist and I was so hard and excited by this he told us that there was a secluded spot up the beach where we could all get completely nude so after a brief talk we decided to try it I got so hard when he removed his swim

Suit exposing a very long thick hard uncut cock to my wife. Her eyes riveted to it he told her to relax and remove her bottoms and I nodded to her that it was ok as I removed mine he then told my wife that her body was so beautifully complimenting her waist m length hair and hard round ass She looked like a young Jennifer Anniston . He then moved very close to her as she lay between us and he gently placed her hand on his big thick cock. As he rubbed oil on my wife's 38 dds I watched as she pumped his big cock in her small hand. His balls bouncing as he fingered my wife he moaned softly and my wife now began to stroke my cock also I was out of my mind with lust and a bit of jealousy because this was brand new to us but I always fantasized About it . My wife Lisa groaned and came on his fingers bucking her hips wildly and this was too much for me I shot a huge load as she pumped my cock and he soon groaned and I watched my wife closely staring as he pumped streams of cum high and onto his belly We put our suits on and he kissed my wife deeply. His tongue going deep into her mouth and asked for our phone number. I wasn't sure about that but this was so incredibly hot that I gave him our number he ended up coming to our home later but that's another story All completely true. In fact this was the start of our wife sharing adventures for many years

# 26. Sexy topless beach adventure 2

We were sunburned and feeling no pain from the drinks earlier at the beach when the phone rang and our Latino friend asked if he could stop by and hang out nude with us for awhile and maybe take some pics of my wife if we'd like.

After consulting with Lisa I gave him the ok and our address. It wasn't long before he arrived and I invited him in and gave him a drink. My wife was wearing short shorts and a thin tank top with no bra and her big tits and hard nipples were clearly on display through the thin material. We drank and chatted about how much fun we had earlier in the day at the topless beach and Carlos asked my wife to pose for some pics for his Polaroid camera(yes this was 1979).Lisa did a couple sexy poses and he instructed her to remove her top and I watched as this handsome Latino man coaxed my young wife into posing with her big tits in various positions and then he had her remove her shorts and do a couple poses and then spread her legs and smile for him as he snapped pics of my sexy young nude wife s ass and open pussy. He removed his shorts and was sporting a big thick hard cock so I did the same. I was out of my mind with lust and felt like I was going to cum without touching my throbbing cock.

Lisa had said that there was to be no intercourse or oral sex as she was unsure about hardcore swapping as we were new to this. I told her anything she agreed on was ok. He agreed with this also. I moved to my wife's mouth as she sat spread out in a recliner and she took my cock in her mouth as Carlos snapped pics. I handed him a dildo and my wife moaned as he slid it into her wet pussy and fucked her with it and snapped a pic. He told my wife to get on all fours and suck me exposing her tight ass to him. Lisa was humping back and forth on the dildo as she sucked me and moaning very loudly.

I asked her do you want a real cock in your pussy baby? She said yes and I said do you want Carlos big cock baby? She deep throated me and said YES and I nodded to him. I watched as he grabbed my wife's hips and buried his thick cock deep inside her pussy. My wife started to orgasm immediately and I shot a big load of cum down her throat and moved to the side .Honestly I felt remorseful and a bit jealous as I sat there with my flaccid cock watching this young Latino stud fuck my new bride like she's never been fucked before. I can't remember how many orgasms she had with him but it seemed like she just kept cumming .You husbands who share know what I mean about remorse after you've emptied your cum and the excitement ebbs. But it didn't take long before; my cock was rock hard again. Carlos began groaning and blurted out to me I'm gonna cum and my wife was also screaming in orgasm and they came together really hard. He filled my wife with so much cum it was running down the inside of her thighs.

They kissed deeply and I slid into my cock into the cummy mess he had made and the feeling of fucking my just well fucked wife and the silkiness of her slippery soaked pussy was a feeling that I was instantly hooked on. I LOVED IT!! I came deep inside her and we rested and agreed to meet again. Carlos kissed Lisa deeply and left. I shared my wife for 15 years afterwards and never got tired watching her enjoy another man's big cock and going last and enjoying her well fucked cum filled pussy.

## 27. My best friend's mom – the next day

I wasn't sure how I should feel after I had just fucked my buddy's mom while his dad watched! It was like the stuff of a porn flick but this really happened! Laura and Rick offered me a place to sleep but I snuck out when I felt I could. I went home and relived this experience repeatedly in my head.

The next morning was Sunday. I got a call from my parents that due to a health issue with my grandfather they would be gone all week and needed me to see if I could stick around. Fortunately I go to a small college so I was able to email my professors and explain my plight. They were really pretty cool about it. Being a good student finally paid off.

I texted Tommy and told him that I would not be going back to campus with him that afternoon. Shortly after I sent that my phone chimed with an incoming message. I opened it to see a shaved pussy spread wide. It was from Laura, my buddy's mom not more than five minutes after I messaged him. She followed up with a message asking if I was okay and said she would see me that evening.

It turned into a chilly, wet, blustery day. I watched football on TV to try to keep my brain occupied with something besides Laura. I happened to glance out the window and it was dusk. I saw a car pull into our driveway. It was Laura and she honked and motioned for me to open the garage door. She pulled in and I went to the short hall that leads to the garage just as she stepped inside. She was wearing a long trench coat. Her perfume filled my senses and I could see a pair of strappy red heels on her feet.

She thanked me for opening the garage door so she wouldn't get caught in the rain. She then grabbed me by the neck of my shirt and pushed me up against the wall and most definitely invaded my personal space before hungrily planting her lips on mine and thrusting her tongue deep into my mouth. I moaned into her as I felt my cock spring from semi-hard to full on boner.

Then Laura quickly broke away and started walking toward the living room. I was in shock and stood there dumbfounded. She looked back over her shoulder as she unwrapped her coat and asked if I was going to follow her or stand there like a dumbfuck. I snapped back to reality and hurried to move behind her as she dropped her coat. As I stepped over the discarded wrap I noticed she was wearing a red satin and lace corset with garter straps, black stockings, and stiletto heels with straps that wrapped around her ankles and lower calves. Her breasts were exposed with hard nipples and no panties to cover her hairless mound and divine bottom.

Laura felt me moving in close behind her. "No, no sweetie. I'm gonna have some fun first. You go over there (pointing) and kneel in front of the sofa." I did as she said as she sat directly in front of me and crossed her lithe legs. She grinned mischievously at me and ordered my to stand and strip totally naked and then kneel again. I stood to get nude in record time when she was stern with me and told me to relax and show down so she could enjoy the visual. I slowed from warp speed and stood there with my erection straight out and then knelt.

Laura looked at me and smiled. She asked if I liked her legs. Then asked if I liked her feet. Finally asked if I liked her shoes. I answered in the affirmative each time. She had easily figured out that I have a fetish for such things. She took the foot of her crossed leg and teased my hardness with her stilettoed foot. I closed my eyes and moaned as I started to leak pre-cum. Laura giggled and then used her foot more aggressively on my cock and balls. She told me that Rick also has the same fetishes and loves to cum on her feet and in her shoes. I just tried to focus on the exquisite feelings in my groin while trying to keep from blowing my load quickly all over the feet and legs of this incredible hotwife.

Laura uncrossed her legs and placed both feet on the floor before ordering me to lick and kiss my way from her toes and up her legs. I worked both of the stockinged feet and ankles as I massaged her calves and crept my way to her knees. I worked my way to Laura's inner thighs and she opened them wider for me until I was tasting the flesh above her nylons and could smell her pungently aromatic pussy. I slid my tongue up the slit of her pussy, splaying it open with my fingers and then flicking her clit with my tongue. Laura moaned and grabbed my hair and pulled me to her pussy with surprising force. She started humping my face as I sucked on her love nub until she yelped with pleasure. I slide two and then three fingers into her wet hole and curled them to try to stimulate her g-spot. I don't know which spot I hit but she started shaking and orgasming like I had never seen a woman do before. As I felt her muscles gradually relax I noticed my face was glazed in a sheen of her cum.

Laura caught her breath and gathered her wits. She stood up and ordered me to do the same. She grabbed my by the cock and pulled it like a handle as she led me upstairs to my bedroom. She pushed me down on the bed and climbed on top of me, slowly lowering herself onto my rigid pole. She sighed and commented about my side as she started rocking in a rhythm with her eyes closed. I reached up and pinched her nipples as she rode me which caused her to change her pace. She started sliding up and down my my rod, slamming he cunt down on me to bury me as deep into her as I could go.

Laura kept pounding on me until she started to make mewling noises and I felt her pussy reach orgasm with a series of convulsions and spasms of her pubic nerves and muscles. Her muscular contractions milked my cock repeatedly until I groaned and let loose with a toe-curling explosion of cum deep into her pussy. I grunted a few more times until the last is my spunk filled her before she fell beside me on my bed, panting together.

As we came back down from our glorious high she informed me that Rick is fine with me being a regular fuck buddy of hers and that they know I'll be home alone all week.

Laura snuggled into me and swung a leg over mine so I couldn't move easily without disturbing her. In a matter of a few minutes one of the most gorgeous women I had ever known was sleeping in my arms as my cum oozed from her.

# 28. Have some time to kill.

From May 2004 to Late November 2007 I shared my wife, first with her co-worker ( he became our Fuck buddy), and with my encouragement and his she fucked 7 men and 3 couples over that time.

It was Cinco de Mayo weekend 2004, after a year of fantasy and flirting this was our first MFM for us and her co-worker. He came in her twice that night. That started a sexual adventure that lasted almost 4 years.

During our third meeting with her co-worker as he was balls deep for the second time that night she moaned over and over "you can fuck me anytime" he ends up unloading in her for the second time.

He rolls off and she is still trembling as she starts to clean him up. I slip in to pure heaven and start fucking her sloppy pussy. I ask her who's pussy is this and she responds " Yours Papi, it's yours but this big chorizo (holding it by the base) can fuck your wife (I start Cumming in her for the 2nd time)anytime he wants". I roll off and she starts to clean me then looks at him and " anytime you want as long as my hubby is there".

That was on a Friday. The following Wednesday we had a lunch date, my wife calls me at first break. "Joe (her co-worker) wants to fuck your wife at lunch" I tell her he needs to call and ask. She hangs up and a few minutes later he's asking me if he could fuck my wife. I still had almost two hours before lunch. Nothing got done.

I head to a park not to far where my wife and I would go once or twice a week for a lunch time quickie, he spied on us a few times over the last year.

My wife told him to ride in front with me as she got in the back. She was naked in a heartbeat. Joe pulled his stiffening cock through his fly.

The whole time in the car my wife kept asking Joe if he's gonna fuck his married co-worker and send her back full. Joe looked at me "Do you mind going first I really want sloppy seconds".

I was in the back and shoved my 6 inches into her soaking pussy, man was she wet. Joe was in the front reaching back playing with her clit then her sensitive nipples, she was cumming in no time, I empty my nuts as her pussy starts to contract.

Since I parked in the most secluded part of this park and the time of day there was only a few cars at the beginning of the park. Joe casually steps out of the passenger side walks around the back with his erection sticking out of his slacks bouncing as he walks. Joe is a taller guy and stood out side as he pulled my wife closer to the door.

he ran his dick up and down her sloppy hole gathering my cum and alternating between slapping and rubbing her clit with his hard cock. She's moaning and begging him to put it in her which he does and slowly sinks balls deep, a few pumps and she starts to cum, he stops, she starts to come down when he starts to pump her hard, I start pinching and twisting her nipples and she goes ape ···· and comes hard that sent Joe over and he started to cum, my wifes eyes go wide then moans out again "he's cumming in your wife Papi. oh fuck, oh fuck".

As he pulls out I notice the big cum stain on his black slacks, my wife pussy was a sloppy mess, my wife takes her thong cleans off Joe and pushes it up her sloppy pussy. I get a call from my wife about 10 minutes before I leave work to go get her. "Papi Joe's cock is hard again, I want it. We only 15 minutes tops, they simultaneously came together in 5, she cleaned Joe with her dress, and Joe left with her thong.

# 29. Fantasy, Reality or blurring the lines

You have been dropping hints to your wife for some time now that you want her to date another. You get turned on when she tells you of her former boyfriends and recently have been stroking to the thought of her dating a hung dom man. It turns your pillow talk into excitement but doesn't seem to go further as she won't discuss it outside of the intimacy of your bed especially since having kids. She has avoided the conversation lately being a little more distant so your head begins spinning when she texts you " be careful what you wish for, don't be late from work today " You try to call her after your meeting but she doesn't answer, your dizzy with confusion and butterflies fill your stomach as you become aroused then calm down not really knowing. You leave work early rushing to avoid traffic, shifting in your seat as you drive getting more and more aroused the closer you get to home. When you pull in you see a car parked in your spot and notice as you enter the kids are gone. You can hear faint noises from the bedroom and as you move towards them you notice her heals and a little further up her shirt, then her bra and as you approach your door you see it is cracked and hear a soft moan – you open the door to see your loving wife kneeling her back to the door as she kisses and gently and passionately sucks my cock into her warm waiting lips. I smile and look up at you, sit down in that chair and do not stroke until we say. As you sit she gets up and kisses you, leaving that after taste of my precum on your lips and whispers " no going back now hon, you wanted this – we are mikes now"

# 30. Last night

My daughter got engaged last week so we hired a pub room for them and laid food on. They invited mostly their friends and some close family.

My wife dressed younger looking thinking she didn't want to be feeling old when it was going to be full of mid 20s people. She had a silver sparkly dress on, thigh length, stockings, tiny thong, black heels, push up bra which should she had cleavage and she smelt so sexy.

Good night had by all and by the end of the night my wife knew all their friends, and had got the attention of several of them, I only bought her 1 drink all night the rest were bought by her new friends. They were all heading to a club and asked her to go with them think I was asked too but wasn't sure it was meant. She declined saying she had to tidy the place as that's what we agreed when we hired it. I told her I'd finish up and she should go out and not very long persuading her she went.

I tidied the room up and the barman pulled me a beer as he was closing up. We chatted he said he hadn't seen it as busy in a while. We chatted a while before I got a taxi and went home.

I sat with a beer watching crap TV waiting for her. Got to 2am and I was falling asleep so went to bed. I was woken at 3.30 when I heard the door close downstairs. I heard voices so stayed in bed.

I listened and it was my wife with a guy, she sounded a little drunk. I heard them laughing and giggling and she said they should go in the lounge as her husband would be sleeping upstairs..

Wasn't long before it went quiet for a bit, I gently creped to the top of the stairs and saw a little light coming from the lounge, the door was slightly open. I heard her saying she liked that and after a while she started to moan a little before saying he needed to get it out.

She commented on how thick it was before what sounded like her sucking his cock. By this time I was hard and stroking listening at the top of the stairs. Noises stopped and I heard her saying that she wanted it inside her, moments later I heard him say how easy its going in as she was soaking before she started to moan.

My wife was being fucked downstairs as I listened upstairs. They were going for it for a while lots of moaning and groaning from my wife and occasional words from him saying what a dirty slag she was. I heard him say he was going to cum she said to fill her but by the sounds of it he pulled out and covered her in it. I heard them kissing and her saying she wanted him hard again.

Went quiet but for the noises of passionate kissing before I heard her moaning again, she must have got him hard and they were now fucking again. It sounded like he was taking her from behind as the noises sounded like he was slapping her ass. She was moaning louder, she kept saying how she liked that and moaned more. I heard her telling him to cum inside her this time but again it sounded like he didn't.

She opened the door came and I shot back into the bedroom, she came upstairs used the bathroom and went back down. Heard him come up and use the bathroom and went back down.

It wasn't long before he was ordering a taxi, Door closed and my wife came up to bed.

She climbed into bed we chatted for 10 mins and she told me

about how he was fingering her pussy in the taxi on the way home and how she wanted his cock. She said she would tell me more about it when she wakes up later. We kissed and I spread her legs and started to lick her pussy but she closed them and told me later.

She has been in bed about 40 mins now and is sleeping, I'm hard waiting for her to wake up and find more details.

# 31. Get Cucked at the B&B

Wives like a few days away every now and then, and alongside some relaxation, there's always room for excitement too - and while some couples enjoy the thrill of possibly finding a stranger in a hotel bar and taking him back to their room, others prefer the anticipation of a pre-arranged meet where there's less left to chance...

So after exchanging a number of messages and photos, you've booked two nights at our B&B, the plan being that if all goes well, I'll be having your wife in front of you while mine's out for a few hours. You arrive mid-evening, and my wife and I show you up to your room - it's fairly spacious, with a distant sea view, but, most importantly, it has a king-size bed, complete with fresh white bedding...

I take the opportunity to admire your wife in the flesh - she's dressed conservatively, appropriate for the journey here, not for what's to come, but is as attractive as in her pics, and I know I'm going to enjoy having her right there in that room, hopefully the next morning. We explain a few things, like where the spare pillows are, and breakfast arrangements, and I mention you're our only guests...

My wife and I leave you to it, and that night I lay awake for an age thinking of what's to come, and hope you're both as eagerly anticipating it as I am - so near, literally the other side of the wall, yet at that point so far! In the morning I'm waiting in the breakfast room, and hear your room door close - looking towards the staircase, I see your wife's bare legs as she makes her way down ahead of you...

She pads into the breakfast room barefoot, wearing a short dress that clings beautifully to her figure, smiles at me as I ask if you've slept well, and grins as she says that the bed's very comfortable. My wife appears behind me, and with a cheery 'Good Morning' asks if you'd like tea or coffee. You settle at your table, your wife crossing her legs and presenting a generous amount of thigh to delight my eyes...

Then she gets up and crosses the room to help herself to some muesli and fruit salad, and smiles broadly when I ask if she needs milk or is a 'smother it in yoghurt kind of girl'! Over the course of the next 40 minutes or so, we engage in casual small talk as the two of you eat breakfast and my wife and I are in and out of the room. All the while I'm eyeing up your wife...

Later, with my wife right behind me, I can tell your wife's restraining herself when I ask if we can get you anything else, and then my wife asks if you have plans for the day - if only she knew! You name a couple of places you're thinking of visiting, but deliberately mention that you're taking it easy and not rushing off anywhere - a suggestion I've made, so my wife doesn't hang around waiting for you to go out...

As you head back off upstairs, I take in the view of your wife's dress clinging to her buttocks as she leaves the room - and come to the conclusion that she's been knickerless throughout breakfast! I tidy everything away and clean up in the breakfast room, and am silently urging my wife to hurry up with the washing-up and cleaning up in the kitchen...

Back in our part of the house, I grow increasingly impatient as she potters about doing bits and pieces, all the while with an increasing sense of anticipation - I'm eager for her to get on and go out, but have to be careful not to show it. Eventually, after half-an-hour or so, she announces that she's off, and a few minutes later she's changed and heads out of the door...

I wait for a couple of minutes in case she's forgotten anything, then head up to your room. I knock the door, and a few seconds later you open it, and I'm greeted by the sight of your wife sprawled seductively on the bed, in a beautiful black lingerie set, teamed with stockings and heels, all of which contrasts perfectly against the white bed linen, and will make for great photos...

"Perfect timing", you tell me as I enter the room, and glancing into the en-suite I see the steamed-up shower, and realise you've spent the time preparing your wife for me. I immediately join her on the bed where we engage in a kiss, and within seconds her hand has drifted to the bulge in my jeans. As she fumbles with the button and zip, you pick up your camera - something we've discussed beforehand...

As she tugs down the front of my pants and her fingers encircle my stiff shaft, I hear the camera click, and you continue to take photos as your wife leans forward to take my cock in her mouth, and suck and lick it. "It tastes as good as it looks, and is as big as it looked too", she mutters to you, presumably referring to the pictures you've shown her of me with other men's wives...

It's been a full week since I've cum, and as she sucks my cock deep into her mouth I warn her she'll soon have me exploding there if she isn't careful - in our email exchanges, you've said she'll want all my spunk in her pussy. She lifts her head immediately, gives me a wicked smile, and whispers naughtily "You'd better fuck me, then!", and lays back, spreading her legs wide...

As I position myself between her thighs, your wife grasps my cock firmly, and pulls me straight into her pussy, which is already soaking wet, despite my not having touched her there yet! She moans softly as I enter her, and pulls me to her for another kiss as I embed myself fully inside her, and from the corner of my eye I see you crouch by the window, from where she and I are being bathed in sunlight....

She hooks her heels behind my knees and takes hold of my hips, pulling me hard into her, expertly squeezing and releasing my cock with her pussy, and I know I'm not going to hold out for long. Sure enough, I soon feel the inevitable surge, and groan out an apology as I explode inside her - pumping spurt after spurt into the depths of your wife's pussy, and I hear you muttering appreciatively....

My orgasm seems to take an age, but when it finally subsides I apologise properly for having cum so quickly, telling your wife she'd felt so good I just hadn't been able to contain myself. She giggles in response, and says it's fine, because ever since arriving, she's been dying to feel my cock and cum inside her! You nod in agreement, and say she was playing with herself during the night...

After a while, my slowly softening shaft starts to slip from her pussy, and as I withdraw and kneel up, some of my spunk dribbles out starts to form a wet patch on the sheet beneath us. As she sits up, she notices it and giggles, saying that I may have cum quick, but have cum lots, and that my wife will think they've been at it like rabbits - and laughs when I tell her I wash all the bed linen!...

"Well you won't have to clean up any more of this mess - that's his job", your wife says, looking directly at you and laying back, and I move aside to give you access to her. In seconds you're on the bed with your face buried in her pussy, eagerly licking and sucking my cum from her. She groans happily as you feast, and pulls your head hard into her, smiling at me as I lay alongside watching...

"You really came a lot, didn't you!", you exclaim, when your wife eventually relaxes her grip on you and you lift your face from her pussy, your lips and chin glistening with the mixture of my cum and her juices. I tell you it was a week's worth, and your wife then says she felt it splashing into her - and pointedly adds that that's not something that happens when you fuck her...

Then, looking straight into my eyes, she announces that seeing as my wife doesn't want it, she'll happily take all of the cum that I can give her during your stay - at which you shuffle out from between her legs, and pick up the camera again as your wife's attention turns back to me. She moves to lean over me, and begins to kiss and lick her way down to my groin....

Looking up directly into my eyes, she licks all around and then along my shaft, which is rapidly stiffening as she runs her tongue up it. "I can taste myself on you", she murmurs, before fully sucking my cock into her mouth. After a few minutes, and satisfied I'm fully re-erect, she shuffles up to straddle me, and turns to ask you why you can't get hard again after you've fucked her and cum.....

Before you even have a chance to answer, she sits straight down to impale herself on my length, gasping as she does so, and I simultaneously let out a groan of pleasure as I feel the hot wetness of her pussy engulf my cock. She gently starts to rock back and forth, and I reach up to fondle and squeeze her breasts, squeezing them and tweaking her nipples...

She whimpers quietly as I roll her nipples between my thumbs and forefingers, and I sit up to suck first one and then the other deep into my mouth, at which she groans loudly. You continue to take pictures as your wife rides me at a steadily increasing pace, and kneel to take close-ups of my cock sliding in and out of her pussy, as she rises and falls on it...

She turns to look back over her shoulder at you, and asks how the view is of her being fucked by a "proper-size cock". Then, telling you you'll get an even better look the other way around, she lifts herself off me completely, swivels around to face you as she kneels over me, hands resting on my thighs, then lowers herself slightly to lodge the head of my cock between her pussy lips...

"Take a good look", she growls, before slowly and deliberately sinking down until I'm fully embedded in her once more. Then, leaning back fully and taking her weight on her hands either side of me, she gradually raises her hips, and I can feel my cock pressing hard against the inner wall of her pussy as she lifts herself up, and she moans in pleasure....

You mutter in appreciation as she almost lets my cock escape, exposing its full length glistening with her wetness, and you take a couple of close-ups before she lowers herself onto me again, and you make sure you capture not just my cock sliding back inside her, but her entire body and face as she looks down towards you at the foot of the bed...

She repeats her actions a few times, slowly and deliberately raising and lowering herself, keeping the just head of my cock between her pussy lips at the zenith, and pressing it firmly against its inner wall as she moves, groaning with the sensation as she does so. "Does his cock feel good, darling?", you ask her, and she looks directly into your eyes as she replies...

"Much better than yours", she says, with a hint of contempt in her voice, "and I'm glad his wife doesn't want it anymore, because it means I'm getting it instead!" At that, she lifts herself off my completely, my cock springing upright as it's freed from her pussy, and she moves to lay on her back alongside me, fingers of one hand encircling my shaft, and virtually dragging me toward her...

Wasting no time, I roll over and position myself between her thighs, and your wife guides my cock straight into her again, and gasps as I push down hard and wriggle against her. "Oh God, that feels so fucking good", she moans softly into my ear as I lay on top of her, and I feel her fingertips dig into my buttocks as she pulls me harder into her....

"Minds the nails!" I whisper, to gently remind her not to leave me with any marks, and she giggles and relaxes her grip a little, but keeps her hands in place. As I begin moving in and out of her, she briefly hooks her heels into the back of my knees again, before lifting her legs up, to wrap them around my waist, and I notice you're back by the window again as you take more photos...

The slight change in position means my cock is pushing slightly deeper into her with each forward thrust, and your wife moans quietly each time I thrust into her. Then, moving her hands from my buttocks and opening her legs wide, she grips my arms, looks up into my eyes, and tells me to fuck her hard and deep. Stopping for a moment, I place first her left leg over my shoulder, then the right...

Looking up at me expectantly, she bites her lip in pleasure as I suddenly push down and into her, and I feel her tense beneath me, before turning her head to look at you. "That feels so fucking good", she exclaims, and for the next few minutes I fuck your wife hard and fast, while you move around the room, taking photos from various angles, until she says she wants me to stop...

I ask if she's OK, and laughing, she replies "I'm not as flexible as I used to be", and moves her legs from over my shoulders, back to where we started, with her heels behind my knees. Placing her arms around my neck, she draws me down to her to engage in a kiss, then clutches me tightly to her as I resume my movements, though slower and more gently at first...

Almost imperceptibly, over the next few minutes I increase the pace, and as I fuck her steadily faster and harder, your wife keeps her arms wrapped around me, and I hear and feel her breathing get heavier, and her body start to writhe underneath mine. "That's it", she groans in my ear, "keep fucking me like that", and then she turns to you, and tells you I'm about to make her cum...

Hearing her say that encourages me to up the pace more, and I start fucking her harder and faster in a concentrated effort to tip her over the edge. "Oh God, oh fuck, yes!", she suddenly cries, and her whole body begins to shake. I continue thrusting hard into her, and then with a loud guttural groan she cums, shuddering violently, and stops me moving by squeezing me in a vice-like grip...

As her orgasm subsides, she turns her head toward you. "Why can't", she gasps breathlessly, "why can't you make me cum like that?", and looks up into my eyes, before pulling me down to engage in another long kiss. Breaking off, she whispers urgently in my ear, "I want to feel your cum in me again", and looks up at me with a glint in her eyes...

I slide my cock from her pussy and kneel up between her legs, and as she rolls over and up onto all fours, I guide her to turn around so she's positioned diagonally across the bed, directly facing the mirror on the wardrobe door, and angled towards you where you're stood in front of the window. She looks back over her shoulder as I shuffle forward to lodge the head of my cock between her pussy lips...

She turns her head back to look in the mirror, and you kneel and take a couple of close-ups of her face as I take hold of her hips and pull her slowly back against me. In the mirror I see her watching herself wide-eyed as I ease slowly all the way into her, and she wriggles her backside to ensure I'm fully embedded inside her, then gasps as I make a short, sharp forward thrust...

I start moving in and out of her slowly to start, but gradually increase the tempo, keeping a firm hold on her hips. She drops her arms to bury her face in the quilt, but soon raises herself to look into the mirror as I increase the pace. As I steadily speed up further, what begin as soft moans get louder, and then turn into groans of "Fuck me, yes, fuck me...."

I'm soon pounding your wife as hard and fast and deep as I'm able, plunging my cock into her pussy, and she grabs handfuls of the quilt, whilst you remain kneeling in front of the window, camera clicking rapidly."Cum in me", she growls, "I want your cum in me", and arches her back, pushing herself hard back into me as I push forward into her and my grip on her hips tightens...

"Give it to her", I hear you mutter, and your wife lifts her face to look up at you as my movements turn to urgent short, stabbing thrusts before a final lunge to lodge the head of my cock in the very depths of her pussy as I feel the second load of cum surging up my shaft. "Oh god, oh fuck, oh yes...", she groans, and stares directly into your eyes as my spunk spurts out into her...

I feel her whole body shaking and trembling as she desperately pushes herself hard back against my groin, whilst I'm simultaneously pulling on her hips to haul her back tightly into me. I swear I can feel the head of my cock straining against her cervix, as my shaft pulsates and spews my seed into your wife, and I groan with a combination of sheer satisfaction and pure pleasure...

As both our orgasms subside, she slowly sinks down to lay facedown on the bed, and keeping my cock inside her I follow, and remain laying full-length on top of her until eventually my shaft slips from her pussy. I roll sideways off of her, and she turns over onto her back, spreads her legs, and tells you it's your turn. "I don't normally get this wet for you, do I?", she asks, and winks at me...

You almost fall over as you rapidly pull down your trousers and pants, freeing your cock, which I immediately see is considerably smaller than mine. "Now you see why I need a proper cock every now and then" your wife giggles to me, as you scramble onto the bed and between her thighs. She reaches down and pulls you into her, and then laughingly asks "Are you in yet?"...

"Yes", you reply, with a look of total pleasure on your face as you start thrusting into your wife rapidly, "and you're so wet and slippery!" She grasps your arms tightly, and hisses "Obviously, because I'm full of Andy's cum", and looks over at me with a broad smile as you groan and let your spunk fly into her. "Mmmm", she moans, in quiet satisfaction...

After you've finished cumming, the two of you embrace tightly, and share a passionate kiss, before you withdraw your cock from her pussy and kneel up between her legs, looking down at her glistening mound. You ask your wife if she's enjoyed herself. "Oh yes", she responds, "and I want more - at least once before we leave"...

I gather up my clothes and start to get dressed, and tell you the room's free for the rest of the week, if you want it. "I'll let you know later for how long", you answer, and looking at your wife I smile, and point out that as I'll need a day's 'recovery time', two more nights might be in order. "At least", she says, smiling back at me as I open the door, "he'll let you know later"...

Half-an-hour later I hear the two of you go out, and not long afterwards my wife comes home. "When did they leave?" she asks, and I tell her I haven't even had time to service your room yet. When we go up a few minutes later and let ourselves in, we find the bed neatly made, and I immediately visualize myself there servicing your wife on it only a short time previously...

That evening, you knock on our door, and when I answer, you ask if your room's free for another four nights. I tell you it is, and over your shoulder I see your wife grinning broadly at me. "That's great", she says, "then can we stay longer, please?". "Of course", I reply, knowingly, as my wife appears behind me, and asks if you've had a good day...

"Lovely", your wife tells her, "just what I needed, wasn't it, darling?" As you nod, my wife tells you she's glad, and is pleased that you're deciding to stay longer. Not half as pleased as me, I think to myself as we bid you goodnight, and later you email me to say your wife's seen there's an Ann Summers shop in a nearby town, and is planning to visit...

In the morning we exchange pleasantries over breakfast, talk about where you went the day before, and what you're planning for the day to come - leaving out any mention, of course, of lingerie shopping! You're out all day, and then the next morning, we follow the same routine as the first, and within minutes of my wife going out, I'm knocking on your room door...

After another couple of hours 'christening' your wife's new outfit by fucking and giving her two more loads of cum for you to clean and then add to, I spend the next day recuperating, before we repeat the pattern the following day. By the time she and I are finished, I'm totally drained, and tell her it's a good job she's not staying longer, because she's worn me out!...

"Well we'll be back, because I want more of this lovely cock!", she growls, fingers encircling my limp, still sticky shaft, before she bends to kiss it. I tell her I'm very flattered, and she giggles "I've never had so much cock and cum inside me, or so often!" When say I've never had bedding with so many cum stains on it, she bursts into laughter, and blames you...

"That's because he doesn't clean up after himself - they're from when he's cum in me after you!", she says, still laughing. As I finish dressing and stand up to leave, you hand me a memory card. "The photos", you say, "let me have it back later". I tell you I will, and transfer them onto my laptop late that evening after my wife's gone to bed...

I slip the card back to you when you arrive for breakfast the following morning, and as on the previous days we hold a perfectly innocent conversation about what you did the day before and have planned for the day to come. "Straight home, sadly", your wife replies to my wife's question about whether you're stopping off anywhere on the way...

When you come back downstairs ready to check out half-an-hour later, I ask if you've anything I can help carry down. "My wife's got a couple of bags", you tell me, and I go up to your room. As I step through the door, she quickly pulls me to her for a kiss. "Thank you", she whispers, rubbing a hand across my crotch, "I really enjoyed myself". "Me too", I reply...

She follows me downstairs, and on returning from taking the bags to your car I hear her talking to my wife as you and I go to process your credit card. "More than alright", I hear her say, in response to my wife's enquiry if everything's been alright during your stay. "The service has been wonderful, absolutely everything we expected, and more!"...

"If only my wife knew what she meant!", I whisper, as I enter the payment amount into the card terminal. "She loved every minute, and so did I", you whisper back, as you enter your PIN and hand it back to me. On reaching the front door, you and I shake hands. "It's been a pleasure having you", I say, and there's a twinkle in your wife's eyes as she looks at me...

"We'll definitely be back", she says, as she steps out of the door, and you wink at me as you follow her out. Shortly afterwards, as I'm stripping the bed, I hold the sheet up to the light from the window, and see half-a-dozen distinct stained areas, and smile at the knowledge that they correspond to the number of times I spurted my cum into your wife...

Later that evening, after my wife's gone to bed, I go through the 150 or so photos that you took, trying to choose the best to upload to my profile whilst preserving your wife's anonymity, in keeping with the agreement made beforehand. As I try to select a variety of shots which also show each of her three outfits, I mentally re-live the moments...

....and reflect that as well as fucking and filling another man's wife six times in three days, I effectively also got paid for the privilege!

# 32. Deja vu

This falls into the long term affair category.

Back in the 80s, I was between wives and living in central California. My brother and his wife of 10 years lived in northern Wisconsin.

I would visit them in the warmer months and they would visit me in the cold months usually for Thanksgiving and/or Christmas. After they had a couple of kids, Christmas was out. They understandably wanted to do Christmas at home.
For several years they pressured me to spend Christmas with them. I demurred. I couldn't see myself going from 60-70F to the snowy frozen north. Finally the pressure was too much and I agreed.

For the life of me I can't remember the name of the town. It sounded like a sneeze! Their house was a huge rambling affair with bedrooms upstairs, HUGE living room/dining room downstairs. There was a smaller room just off the living room where they had their television. It had a working wood fireplace that turned the small room into an oven.

Anyway, my brother's wife made a potent drink for the holidays. She was from India, and the drink was a version of mead. In the Indian version, they added ground or distilled marijuana bud and leaves, milk and various spices. In my sister in law version, she added mead, fermented honey to it. It is a tasty drink that will knock you on your butt.

Sooo, Christmas Eve night they put the kids to bed so Santa can come. The three of us spent the evening putting out the presents and imbibing this potent drink. We ended the evening sitting in the small TV room with a fire going trashed! We were in PJs. The plan was to watch a little TV then call it a night.

My brother and his wife get frisky their playing grabass. He's trying to get her to flash me, etc. etc.

Ultimately we're all drunk enough that she does. She had and has nice tits. Maybe 34C then; maybe 36C to D now. She was and is a petite thing, 5' 1" or so 100-110 pounds then. Maybe 50 pounds heavier now.

Anyway, my brother was playing with her tits and I objected. I had no tits to play with. Playfully, drunkenly SHE said I have two. You can each have one.

The inevitable happened. We went from sucking her jugs to feeling her up to a drunken threesome. We did spit roast, one on ones, you name it we did it.

Christmas morning we're all embarrassed but with the excitement of Christmas, we never talked about it.

Long story short, for the next 20 years or so there were repeats of that night. It would happen 2 to 3 times a year. She told us she really looked forward to it. She was a virgin when she and my brother met so this was very exciting for her.

Over time, she became a sexual animal. The three of us went to nude beaches, swingers clubs, etc. It was a fun time in all of our lives. Aside from the normal competition between brothers there was little to no jealousy.

Anyway, my brother dies and she and the kids move to India to be close to her family. We tried to stay in touch but with time and the distance, we lost touch.

Five years later, I'm still in California but a different town. I'm sitting in bar on Monterey Bay. My brother's ex with her new husband are in the states and we bump into each other. They were doing what I call the Highway 1 tour, Big Sur, Hearst Castle and points south ending at Disneyland.

Her new husband knew I was her ex-brother in law but knew nothing about our escapades. I invite them to my place for an impromptu BBQ. She and I manage to hook up after her husband goes to sleep.

She and I are old farts now. We Skype routinely. They are planning another trip to the states and they're staying with me. I can't wait!

# 33. Not my intention.

It was not my intention to have my wife fuck another man let alone a co-worker of hers who was blessed with a cock my wife became addicted to.

Liz had always been a thick girl, standing at 5' even, her 36 Ds and Phat A$$, 34 inch waist. She looked like a thick Gloria Estefan. Liz always was a natural flirt and really enjoyed showing a lot of cleavage and shaking that Phat A$$ of hers.

Being her best friend I knew she was on the pill and was fucking her Boyfriends brains out every chance she got, loved the feeling of cum in her, especially if she has to go out in public and talk to people. I was the second to enjoy that for a year. She was horny all the time, she blamed her super sensitive nipples for that.

I found out why, they're round like nickels and protruded about an inch, sensitive enough for her to orgasm from playing with them, and if her bras weren't padded they would poke through and be clearly seen. "If you can get to my nipples, my pussy is yours".

Due to her heavy periods her mom got her on the pill at a young age to lessen the pain and flow, she would screw her BF brains out on a daily basis. During her period she was a horny bitch. He took her A$$ and she loved it.

We lost contact over the 2 years she was gone. Ran into her at a mutual friends party, She was with her boyfriend. She gave me a big hug and a very nice kiss on the lips which her boyfriend didn't like.

Later that night we fucked in the back yard while her boyfriend was watching a UFC. I have her bent over a table her dress around her skirt hiked up. It was quick , once I hold of her nipples she came, I told her I was ready, she pushed me off and squatted and took my slick 6 inches down her throat as I unloaded a weeks worth of jizz. She swallows, (mmm I miss that, he doesn't like this" she said as she kissed me and stuck her tongue in my mouth.

She dumped him the next week and we got back together. So during tht time she tells me she had sex with 3 more men and her last one was the biggest at a little over 7 inches but not the thickest she says.

One of them liked, teddies, body stalking's, and garters and thigh highs, which she loved to wear when we would go out. One got her comfortable wearing sheer bras on nights out dancing. She was always comfortable in her 4 inch stilettos.

Fast forward we marry, by now we've introduced a 7 inch thick dildo and vibrator and a lot of porn. Most of my friends stopped going out with us, due to their wives pissed with my wife flirtatious ways and bumping and grinding on them on the dance floor.

So it all started with me trying to boost my wife confidence after the birth of our child.

After the birth of our child Liz hit a bad bit of depression. She hated that her tits grew to a DD and her light brown areolas and nipples turned to a much darker brown and her nipples were a little thicker.

After about 8 months I enrolled her in a TaiBo Class that opened up a few block from us. Between that and dieting she went from a size 22 to 16 and looked great. Sex was picking up but she was still down.

A lady she befriended at TaiBo hooked her up with an interview for a receptionist position that she nailed. It turned out she was replacing her friend who was retiring. This would be the first job Liz had with people more our age as her previous jobs she the youngest by 20 years. Her friend even got the company to give her a $500 dollar signing bonus for a new wardrobe. The lady even told her not to be to shy and show off some of that momma cleavage it helps around there.

We went shopping and she still stayed away from sexy panties and most of her work clothes showed minimal cleavage. She started blowing me again so things were looking up.

She keeps on working out and know she's a size 14. She's happier but still pissed that her beautiful tits are so dark and ugly. I thought they were sexy and couldn't keep my hands of them. Since she was still nursing she wouldn't let me suck them.

Her new dress were showing a bit more cleavage. She gets down to a size 12 and looks amazing, but still does not feel sexy or desirable. Her friend was so proud of her that she gave her $300 Fredericks of Hollywood gift card. With that I talked into her getting some Garter belts and various stalking, thongs and a couple sexy bra and panty sets.

I picked out some work clothes for her. She was wearing knee length and longer skirts and dresses to this point. the ones I picked were about 3 inches above her knee, her dresses and blouses showed off a lot more then she had but still respectable. She had been wearing pumps, I got her 4 pairs of 4 inch CFM pumps. She was not to keen on changing it up for work but after her sister showed up and had a fashion show, her sister reinforced my sentiments and told her she looked like total MILF and Show it off.

We started going out and she was turning heads and I told her so. That seemed to help as she gave me road head and let me fuck in our car port. We started spending our hour lunches fucking 2-3 times a week. Though she still had moments where she would be really down and not feel desirable no matter what I did.

She gets promoted to 8 person department, during this time we have only one car. and I'm working about 2 miles from her, we carpool and spend our hour lunch together at a park near her work. I was pleasantly surprised when she wanted to fuck at lunch like we used to do.

So when I pick up Liz, she has to wait up to 15 minutes for me to get there. Her first day on her job I see her sitting with this tall man standing next to her looking down her top I'm sure.

I pull up and as he opens the door for my wife, she introduces him as Joe her trainer and the man she's replacing. I'm not jealous but I do know when some one is checking out my wife. I'll admit he was cool about not to obvious, but being a perv myself I knew this guy was peeping on my wife.

Things are looking up , she's wearing thongs, and the heels but will not put on the new bras, she did start wearing the garters on nights we went out so I wasn't going to push it.

We're having lunch twice a week with 4 of her co-workers Joe being one them, two other females and a 21 your old guy Danny who flirts with Liz when no one was round she would tell me. Out of the 8 co-workers 5 of them were married including Joe. They would do Happy hour was every Friday at a Mexican Restaurant that featured a DJ that started at 8. Liz always refused the invites.

Her 6 month training was coming to an end and they talked her into going to happy hour to celebrate.

Since we had to go home first and wait for a sitter I talked Liz into changing as I wanted to stay for the DJ and get our groove on, which she happily agreed. Mini Skirt, bare legs and a deep plunging blouse and to my surprise she put on one of the sexy bras. She loved the cleavage but hated the fact her nipples were on point. A little medical tape made a smaller mound instead of a pyramid.

WE show up an hour late and all eyes were on her when we arrived. Hugs for everyone, the women complemented her on her sexiness. By the time the DJ started most of the co-workers split, leaving the other 2 women and the Danny.

All of us danced together and I could not help notice the 21 year old keep talking into my wife's ear and she would smile then come dance with me a bit. She told me he was complementing her on her change of clothes,not saying his exact words. I noticed she had a familiar swag for the next few days.

I had a Monday off, Liz asked me to take our kid in to see mommy's work and meet the team. The way the cubicles are set up, Joe cube opens to my wife's acorns the way. At one point I ask my wife for something, she went for her purse in the bottom draw. She turns half way and reaches for her purse I notice Joe looking at a perfect shot at my wifes tits, specially some of the tops that hang a bit when she bends over. I couldn't be mad at him , I would have done the same thing.

At one point I leave the office and on my back in, I see Liz bending over picking a toy up and Joe squeezing his crotch under his desk. Funny how fast he scooted his chair in when I went by.

At this point I just thought of him fascinated with her big tits like everyone else and didn't really think about him wanting to fuck her. We started doing happy hour every other Friday and Joe did as well. She started getting comfortable enough to wear her sexy bras, she would still tape down her nipples.

Since our condo was between work and the happy hour spot we always went home to change and see our kid before heading out for the night. This particular evening her mom picked up our kid and left quick to beat the traffic back to Riverside.

Liz shocked me when she ask me to roll a joint as she got ready, before she dressed and put on her lipstick we took shot and smoked the J. I layed out the Garters and matching bra and thong set. She put them on and taped her nipples down, I tried to talk her out of it, but she would not hear it. In the car I notice I could see the top of the stalking tops, Liz noticed and just said she had to be a bit careful when sitting and dancing. I ask her again in the car and she says nothing. We pull in, "Give me a minute" she says. I get out, tie my shoes then I open her door, I see her nipples straining, making a small pyramid out of her blouse, she tosses the tape away and gives a small peck while slipping the tip of her tongue between my lips, instant hard on.

Drinks were flowing, the DJ has been playing for an hour or so, she has daned numerous times with Joe the Danny (21yr old) and a 40 something year old milf that stayed. After 2 straight songs where my wife and Tara (40 something milf) were dirty dancing with all of us Joe left for the Restroom, I followed a few minutes after. I didn't see him at the urinals, then I heard a moan it sounded s if someone jacking off, then Danny walks in, and hears the same thing and says "Joe you in there beating your met or what".
joe came out a little flushed,, I 'm pretty sure he was in there beating off thinking of my wife. Right there was the first time I thought about Joe or anyother man fucking my wife.

All weekend I was thinking of Joe checking out my wife at work and fucking her at lunch like I do. I started thinking if him fucking when I was. I was using the dildo on her thinking it was Joe. We started doing DPs with dildo in her twat and me in her A$$, I always would imagine it was Joe.

I didn't think it was normal for me to want to watch Joe or any other man fuck my wife, but rationalized it was ok dress my wife sexy to unknowingly flash him at work.

I decided to first tell her about Joe peeping her which she did not believe. I told her to pay attention when she goes for purse or how many times he stops by her desk for nothing. What I didn't tell her was my new desire to see her fuck him.

The next morning I drop her off and before he could get to the door I tell her pay attention. She calls me at first break and tells me I'm right, he's a pig. And Tell her no it's that you're a MILF, and I remind her how she used to enjoy teasing and flashing.

We fucked at lunch and then had a serious talk on the way home and later that evening. I encouraged her to tease him since he's getting shots anyways. She was reluctant, then after some serious pussy eating and some dp with dildo, we're laying there and she asked me what I had in mind.

It was simple. I lay out what to wear and you wear it. Other than normal views he gets, it's up to you how much more he sees.

Basically if it wasn't windy or Rain Liz would always be in a dress or skirt. I started buying the tiniest G-strings, Crotch less panties, body stalking's, and 1 black sheer bra. It took a bit to get her to start wearing the sheer bra. Liz loved how the crotch less style really let her longer than average lips feel unconstrained.

The first week we're both nervous and excited, I started slow; it was cold that week so I chose a long sleeve black thong style teddy, tight jeans, and her knee high boots with 4 inch heel.

Liz bent down to pick our kid and the thong came into view, before I could tell her she put on a light sweater so I assumed she knew so I said nothing. She looked great, we dropped off our kid at the sitters, she forgot her key card so we went back home, I couldn't help, once in the condo I came from behind and cupped bot tits, worked one hand in her bra and took hold off her engorged nipple as she ground her phat A$$ into me, it didn't long for her to pull her pants down unsnap the teddy and bend over the arm of the sofa. I wasted no time and was in her balls deep, I'm tweaking both nipples as she's grinding herself into me, she comes hard , I tell I'm close, she pushes me back and squats and swallows my rock hard 6 inches and takes may load. She comes up gives me a kiss and fixes her teddy and off we go. As Joe opens the door for her she tells me " Breakfast was great she wants' the same for lunch".

I pick her up for lunch and Joe wanted to go but Liz shot him down. She was joking about it as she's stripping out of her jeans. The park is about 5 minutes away and has a nice secluded spot towards the back.

We're going at it, I'm holding her nipples as her big tits bounce, she's moaning out she's going to cum, I don't know why but I moan out " I bet Joe would love this lunch" she looked me right in the eye as her pussy starts to contract she's bucking, she starts crying out "Fuck Yea" over and over as I start to cum in her. WE didn't have anything to clean up so when I pulled out she took care of that for me, she started to straighten up and told me she would clean up in the gym. As I stepped out I noticed Joe's car leaving our little area (he started doing that every time we went. I didn't mention that to her. Nothing was said about my comments for about a month.

In that time I started taking her panties at lunch on the days we were out with her co-workers and encouraged her to flash Joe. It was all up to her if she wanted to go through with it.

Danny was really laying it on thick with compliments and even apologized in advance if he says anything inappropriate. Again all of us would dance and the girls would rotate round the guys, Joe would back off a bit specially when Liz tried to grind her A $$ on him, Danny on the other hand took as many liberties he could get away with. Like taking hold of her hips as she grinded her as into his crotch, caress her sides , or slap her ass. At the end of the night she was ready to fuck in the parking lot. Normally I would be in it in a heartbeat, but I had rented an all MFM 3 sum porn.

My dick had been hard most of the night, I had her pull her top down and play with her tits as we drove home, she came good just as we're pulling into the carport. My cock is rock hard, I open the door she's sitting now with her dress hiked up her tits out, her panties are soaked. I help her out and turn her around and bend her over the passenger seat, Hiked up her dress and even with poor lighting I could see her glistening pussy lips hanging from her bush.

I slipped in and slowly fucked her for a minute or two before pulling out.

We go inside I start the video and eat her pussy to two orgasms as she watched a house wife take on her hubby and his co-worker. We started going at and during the second scene the wife is getting DPd by two of her co-workers. I tell her sit on the dildo your getting DPd like the movie

Again as I slip into her butt and start sliding in and out feeling the fake cock and my wife moans as I pick up the pace I again moan out " I bet Joe would love to be that dildo" she starts to work the dildo with a little more vigor as I go for her nipples, the sensations to much for me and I start to cum in her A$$, that did it, she pulls off me, with my dick still shooting its last spurt she rolls over on to her back and starts slamming her pussy with the dildo, never saying his name but crying out " fuck me, oh yea fuck me till you cum" with that she held the dildo fake balls deep as I started suck on her nipples, " I'm fucking Cumming all over your cock" she cries as she gives her spasming twat a few more pumps before letting slip out from her, covered in her juice.

She looks at me " What the fuck was that about, the MFM porn my comments, are you trying to tell me something, you want to fuck other bitches".

I finally told her I heard Joe jacking off after dancing with her and that ignited a fantasy of me wanting DP her for real, I left out the part when he's been following us to the park.

She was opened minded enough to accept the fantasy and even call the Dildo Joe. My cock was hard after the two hour conversation and she noticed it. She swings her legs over so we're in 69, "Papi why don't you let Joe fuck me while your there" she says as she hands me the dildo. So that's basically how we would end our happy hour nights.

One happy hour I back in to a spot where no one can park on the passenger side, there was a wall. After an evening of dirty dancing we were both ready to fuck, we're walking to the car and she's telling me she can't wait and needs my cock in her.

I unlock the car and she opens the back seat and bends over and hikes up her skirt and pulls her G-string to the side. It's pretty dark and I have a good view of oncoming people. It lasted about 5 minutes, once back at the condo she tells me to get Joe we're not done yet.

after a couple of happy hours like that, Joe started to park in that spot, so I backed in right next to him. Liz was horny as normal and wanted dick, this time I had in the front seat with sun visor on I pulled off her dress and thong, I left the thong on his side mirror, I cracked the passenger side windows a bit and slipped into her wet pussy. I had drank more then I should it took almost 15 minutes for me to bust and Liz enjoyed two orgasms and was not quiet about it. I heard the car start and leave about 10 minutes into it, WE both came and she asked for her panties. I had to open the door to step out and noticed her G-strings were hanging from my side mirror, I grabbed them and they were warm and gooey, I stuffed her G-string gooey from Joe's jizz into my wife's twat. Not even thinking he might have an STD. Once in the car port she looks at me and pulls the panties and starts sucking the juices from it. My cock went rigid, we ended up ending the night in a dp as she sucked n her G-string. After we finish we're making out and she tells me how she loves the taste of our juices on our tongue, with all the action it slipped my mind that she had just sucked Joes cum from panties and I was just sucking on her tongue.

Sex was hotter than ever, both of us were enjoying the benefits of the flashing and teasing. Liz even gave Danny a couple of titty shots.

One morning I laid out a white crotchless panty garter set, she loved the way it held her bush back and how it framed her pussy perfect leaving her long lips exposed.

As we enter the parking lot I raised her skirt a bit so her lace tops were showing, Liz looked at me "your bad" My reply was , what does that make you? " NAUGHTY" she says.

Before Joe could get to the door Liz rolls down the window and he bends down to look at me as, I start to talk to him, he had a hard time keeping his eyes on me after seeing the lace tops. He eventually opened the door and when I saw his eyes go wide as my wife stepped out and her skirt rises higher, I knew he just got a great shot of her lips. He walked with his briefcase in front of his crotch in to the office behind her.

I had barely sat at my desk when Liz calls and confirmed he got a eyeful and it was my fault. I asked how she feels and she admitted she was embarrassed and excited. More embarrassed about her bush, she never shaves, she'll have me trim her twice a month or she'll get it waxed for very special occasions. And definitely excited because he didn't go straight to his desk and knows it was her that made him feel that way.

I pick her up and Joe walks her to the car and opens the door like he normally does, Liz get back in, she's talking to me, I've got sunglasses on so Joe can't see me staring at him looking my wife's crotch, it was a long 2-3 seconds, his eyes were bigger than earlier. As were pulling away I look between spread legs and see her lips were parted and glistening. I had no doubt Joe was jacking off somewhere.

We have SUV now with Limo tint back windows, I park, set up the sun visor, Liz is naked by now laying back massaging her tits. I leave the back window cracked a bit, with the AC on and the radio we can't hear much outside.

We have about 45 minutes before we had to get ready to back. So I take some time and eat my wife to a loud orgasm, As I get up to mount her I see Joe's car, he parked across from us. I started pumping her and telling her how sexy she was and how wet she is.

I tell her it's from Joe seeing your wet lips spread open, and you liked it. She looks me straight in the eye and starts gyrating her hips and cries out she's cumming, I tell her i'm close and she moans out not to cum in her, a few moe pumps and I pull out and crawl up , she leans forward and gets half my cock in her mouth as I start to cum. I throw my head up and see Joe heading back to his car quick.

Liz starts cleaning up and then says " To answer your?,I like it just as much as you do Papi".

We skipped a few happy hours to do our own thing. There was an El Torito in Fullerton that had a small dance floor and played our type music we like to dance to. One night after as we're watching MFM porn and using Joe (the dildo) as our third, again I'm in her A$$ and fake Joe is stuffed in her kitty. I get a hold of her big nipples and she saying how good two cocks feel in her, she can't believe she's fucking her co-worker. As she starts to cum I ask her if she wants to try the real thing, she's on her knees leaning forward on one arm, she's fucking herself harder with fake Joe and crying out for the both of us to fill her holes as she's cumming. I cum hard in her butt and roll off and clean up as she rolls over with fake Joe still buried in her.

"No way, we agreed it's just a fantasy". The next morning as were laying there she says "what makes you think he wants fuck me, besides he's married". I tell not worry, there's no way you would try the real DP, it's cool.

Joes B-day was coming up, his family was in Puerto Rico, So I suggested we invite him to shoot some pool. Our kid wasn't feeling well so Liz stayed as I met up with Joe.

After a couple pitchers, I confronted him about spying on us, he straight out told me, after the thong on his side mirror and all the flashing he couldn't resist and he apologized if we were pissed.

I told him of my fantasy and if he could keep his mouth shut and play along then maybe he can help make it a reality. I tell him she can't know that I filled you in, I can't promise you anything other than teasing and flashes your getting now.

He agreed, I started giving him advice on what her turn on were, like he should touch her hand, arm, or even her knee when he talks to her. And definitely be more touchy on the dance floor, don't be scared to smack her ass when she grinds on you, grab her hips and pull her into you, stuff like that. I tell him Liz is a big girl and if Liz doesn't like it shell stop it nd tell you.

Liz would bring up trying the real during sex. The seed was planted.

The first happy hour where Joe took a lot more liberties with Liz had her make a major decision. I had told Joe before hand to make sure he sits next to Liz and Cadillac Margaritas are her favorite.

It was pretty warm that night, Liz asked what she should wear. Lakers are playing so something Lakers and go commando. She came down in a Jean mini skirt and a Laker shirt that had an over sized neck line that hung off the one shoulder a bit. She had on the wedge heels and looked hot.

Liz asked for a shot so we had a couple before leaving.

We walk in and spot them at a table next to the dance floor with 2 chairs next Joe. Liz and I walk the table and she hugs everyone as I just hug the women and shake Danny's hand, she got to Joe last, after a hug Joe pulled out the chair for her. Joe wasted no time and leaned with his hand on her knee and told us he already ordered the first round.

2 hours of drinking when the DJ started. No one was feeling any pain. WE all started dancing together, first it was Liz and the other two ladies doing some dirty dancing before both had to go since they drove together. That left us with Danny and Joe.

Danny was talking into her ear again, this time Liz would back off shake it for him a little then waves no, no with her finger. She gets to me and she's hot and sweaty her nipples are at attention so I know she's turned on. She gets to Joe, first they're facing each other swaying then the song changed to a booty shaker, she spun around and started to bump and grind when Joe took hold of her hips and started a little bump and grind of his own, it didn't take long for Joe to pull away and sit down. Danny and I sandwiched my wife with her A$$ against Danny. Liz looks at me in the eyes the whole 2-3 minutes as Danny caressed her sides and even cupped her tits for second before Liz spun around and the song ended. Danny had a booty call and had to go, he gave my wife big hug and looked like he squeezed her A$$.

Liz went to the restroom as I ordered our last round. When she came back she sat on Joes lap for a minute gyrating to the music before getting up an sitting on my lap, she slipped off her sandals and placed them on Joes lap. Liz loves her feet rubbed, I didn't even think of tell Joe that. So when he wrapped his big hands around her foot she melted back into me, I knew Joe had to get a beaver shot the waitress brought her out of the trance. We finished our drinks as Joe kept his hand on my wife's thigh for the next 30 minutes or so.

I went to the restroom, on the way back I saw them on the dance floor, I watched her facing him swaying and leading him toward the darker side of the floor which I had a perfect view as he was now caressing her sides like Danny was earlier, she spun around, she reached back to put her hands around his neck, he starts to caress her waist, I headed to the dance floor and saw him cupping both tits before sliding his down back to her hips.

He said he had to go and left pretty quick. She pulls me into her, "you need to take me out to the car and fuck your naughty wife".

I leaned her against the wall and kissed her hard as I ran my hand up her thigh and found her inner thigh slick with her wetness and her lips soaked I easily slipped two fingers in her before we walked out. My cock was straining in my pants, I could not get her to the car fast enough.

At the car she was quick to bend over the back seat, I was in her and first thing I did was to get her out of that bra. with both hands full of thick nipple, she moaned out "Fuck me, fuck your naughty wife" I start pumping her and tweaking her nipples like she loves she moaning and telling me how she felt Joes cock throb on her A$$, she then tells me as he cupped her tits she felt him throb a lot and thinks she made him nut. I started cumming in her and she cried out again as she started to orgasm. It was over in less than 5 minutes.

I stepped back and Liz turned and swallowed my dick, cleaning it like she used to.

At home I put on the MFM porn and Liz grabbed fake Joe and was already sliding into her before the first scene started.

We're going at it, Joe in her pussy an me in her ass, between the moans and fuck me she says "Papi I want to feel two real cocks double fucking me". I couldn't believe what she just said. My cock swelled and I pounded her A$$ hard for a good minute or two, and came hard in her, Liz was right behind and cried out loud she was cumming on both our cocks.

The next morning I let her sleep in, I couldn't wait to see of she was serious about brining Joe into our sex life.

The next morning I have coffee brewing, I'm thinking about how this all started with me wanting to boost Liz's confidence to flashing her co-worker Joe, to wanting to DP my wife with her co-worker Joe, then it dawned on me she agreed to do it last night. Instant erection.

I went straight to bed. I spooned with her, she was still wet from earlier, I easily slid into her when she gyrated her hips. I caressed her hips as she contracted her pu$$y with little gyrations and light moans. I worked up to her exposed tit and started rolling her nipple causing her to start to moan more and gyrate her hips a little more, pinching her nipple harder like she likes it she starts pushing her a$$ back on me, I lift her leg and start fucking her, I get her on her back, with her legs over my shoulders I started to fuck her hard.

There were no words spoken just grunting, groaning, moaning, and the sounds of slapping skin and her sloppy pussy. I loved it.

I moan out I'm close as I'm pounding her, she moans into my ear " You going to handle watching Joe fucking me like this". I pushed up and slowed my pounding to a hard thrusting, I'm balls deep exploding into her, looking straight into each other's eyes, and she goes into her orgasm. Her pussy contracts so hard it pushes me out with a flood of her juices.

Laying there she tells me, she's sure Joe nutted in his pants when he cupped her tits and felt her thick hard nipples he groaned in her ear and felt his cock throbbing, that's when he split quick.

"If we are going to do this you are going to ask Joe to come and join us and fuck your wife, Your not going to throw it in my face later and want to fuck other bitches, or get mad jealous after it starts.". I agree and tell her if we do this No kissing on the lips and no anal, that's only for me, she agreed.

Liz did say she'll do it but she's not ready just now, she'll let me know when I can have that talk with Joe not knowing I already have been having that talk with Joe.

That was in August of 2003, Joe didn't get his chance till May 7, 2004 after happy hour.

During those 9 months Joe and I became friends. He even introduced me to his wife, and then I understood his fascination with Liz, she was very similar to Liz when she was a size 22, just not as pretty and lacked the T&A Liz was blessed with. She never met Liz as she never went to company events.

Joe and I would go play pool and would talk about Liz and what he can do to better his chances. I would tell him she likes to be treated like a queen in public and slut in the bedroom and just keep doing what he's doing. He did mention he was in a rocky marriage as she caught him cheating on her with a co-worker. He was quick to say it was a very short affair.

# 34. Austin Tx

It happened in Austin

Normally when you see an adventure I or my wife posted it involves my wife. This past week while on a business conference to Austin Tx I had my own adventure.
Yes it's true and there is no Bi content and no pictures to share.

Once a year my employer sends a representative from the office to the National conference for a week. This year it was held in Austin. It's a meet and great type of event with a lot of boring lectures and new product reviews during the day and a lot of drinking in the evenings... I'm not much for the bar scene. Prefer a good glass of wine or cold beer with dinner and relax. Something unusual in my profession. I know boring.

Wednesday night I was enjoying a nice meal and my own company when I noticed a lady from the conference setting alone at a nearby table. She seemed to behaving a bit of a heated debate with someone on her cell. There was a lot of texting and throwing her phone on the table then a call and finally she says fine if that's what you want I will and hung up. . I know it was none of my business but couldn't help myself? I ask if she was ok. She apologized for interrupting my meal with a argument with her husband. I told her no problems; my wife and I had been there a time or two and understood. She laughed and said she doubt we had had this disagreement before.

I laughed and told her after 40 years of marriage I doubted there was anything that we had not debated at some point and if she wanted to talk about it I would listen. I offered desert and another glass of wine that she accepted. She relaxed and we enjoyed each other's company. The conversation was about work the conference and family before it turned to her call. You could tell she was a bit embarrassed, may it was the wine but she started to explain.

When her husband of 18 years found out she would be attending this conference alone he encouraged her to use a hall pass and get some as he said strange and let loose. The closer the conference came the more he talked about it. Telling her different situations he would like to happen. Texting him pictures, calling him etc. She Always said no. The conversation I witnessed was about the same subject. With a grin I reminded her that she told him she would before she hung up on him. She blushed and said she didn't know I heard that part. At this point we had been talking a couple hours and the waiter was giving us the eye like it's time to leave. We left him a nice tip and went back to the hotel. In the lobby I thanked Her for those company and as a joke I gave her my business card and wrote down my room number on the back in case she changed her mind and we went our separate ways. I called my wife as I did every night and let her know about my dinner date and never though any more about it. The conference was having a closing activity/party Thursday evening and I was flying home Friday afternoon.

Thursday night I get a text from an unknown number with an attached picture. It was a selfie of my new friend with my hotel room # in the back ground and a message asking if I was available for another conversation. I opened the door to a very nervous Anna and a bottle of wine.

Gone were the previous night business cloths and looking very comfortable in Jeans and tank top. Very pleasing to the eyes. I invited her in an apologized for the condition of the room.

I got a couple of glasses and poured us a drink. She was quite just looking at her glass when I broke the silence and ask what she wanted to talk about. She said that after she got back to her room last night her husband called again. Apologized for being a jerk. She told him about meeting me and some of our conversation. He wanted to know if she was serious when she said she will use her hall pass. He said he was just wanting her to enjoy herself and really let lose. Also how it would be a big turn on for him if she did and shared it in some way. She had been thinking about it all day and that's what leads her to my door.

She said if I was willing maybe I could take a couple pictures with her phone and that would give him something to jerk off too and wonder what she was doing.

How could I say no. I told her we could do a story with pictures starting with the one she took of my room # and take as many or as few as she wanted. How far it would go was entirely up to her. She sent him the one of the room # and a message "last chance to change your mind before I knock on the door. His response "go for it". With that response she seemed to relax more and decided to" go for it"

The next picture was of me standing in the doorway then a selfie of the two of us together. Then sent them to him. I kissed her and she backed away. I thought I went too far too fast. Then she kissed me this time with far more passion. It was a lover's kiss and another selfie sent of the kiss. We made out for a few minutes; I was able to get a hand under her blouse to play with a tits, when her phone went off. Yep his timing was lousy. She told him to stop texting she was busy and would send him messages when she was done fucking her new friend.

We talked some more. I impressed on her that sometimes fantasy is better than reality. While I was more than willing to take this as far as she wanted she needed to think of the end result with her husband.

She pulled her top off and tossed it in the floor and ask if I wanted her to take her bra off. Silly question.

She turned her back to me and removed her bra. It was tossed with her shirt. She hesitated for a minute before turning around. She was Beautiful with the nipples as fat as my thumb and standing tall. Before she had a chance to say anything I kissed her and we took up where we left off. We worked our way to the bed kissing and exploring each other like a couple of teenagers. I managed to get my hand in her pants and she was soaked.

I ask how much further did she want to take this. She got up and took a picture of her blouse and bra and my shirt in the floor and sent it to him. Followed by a topless selfie with me in the back ground. She handed me her phone and ask that I take some more pictures as she stripped. She was really getting into the picture story for her husband. I took several pictures of her getting undressed and adding the cloths to the previous pile. Once naked she was on the bed posing . Everything from tasteful nudes to legs spread showing me (and hubby) a recently well trimmed bush. We laid in bed together talking and sending the pictures to her husband as we made out naked on the bed. He called her again, as they were talking I started chewing on her nipples and working my way down to her pussy. She was still talking to hubby I slid one then a second finger into her pussy as I sucked on her clit. She let out a moan and dropped the phone and grabbed my head. I was licking and sucking and she was humping my face. She cam all over my face. I could hear her husband wanting to know what was going on. She grabbed the phone and took a picture of my head between her legs and sent it then said she could not talk any more there was a dick that needed sucked and hung up.

She handed me the phone and said no matter what happens don't stop taking pictures. I tried as best as I could as she started sucking my dick. I got pictures of her looking at the camera with my dick in her mouth. She knew what she was doing and it wasn't long before I told her if she didn't stop I was going to cum. She didn't stop and neither did I. I Unloaded a week's worth in her mouth and on her face and tits. She laid with her head on my thigh next to my limp dick with cum on her face and took a couple of selfies. Then started sending them to her husband while I got us a towel to clean up a bit. She said these pictures will push him over the top, I have never let him cum in my mouth before. Tits, yes but I never swallowed. You were my first.

We cleaned up a bit. She didn't bother to get dressed or act like she wanted to leave so I pulled her in close and we talked about nothing and everything. We played and caressed but never mentioned her husband or answered his text. After a bit she started sucking my dick again. She was not trying to get me off just enjoying sucking and licking my limp dick. It was not long before I was hard. No words were said as she lowered her wet pussy on my dick. Damn she was tight and it took a couple minutes to get all the way in. Once there she leaned her head back and slowly rocked back and forth. Her tits were swaying and she was smiling. I picked up her phone and took a couple more pictures of my dick as in went deep in her pussy and her tits swaying back and forth. His text was still open so I sent them with a note thanking him for the pleasure of his wife. She rode me till she cam then rolled over on her back. I got between her legs and fucked her till we both cam.

She spent the night with me we fucked a couple more times that night with a lot of playing and pictures in between. She would send them to him throughout the night just so he knew she was staying with me. In the morning she woke me by sucking on my dick. When I was ready to cum she pulled away and had me cum on her face first then sucked the last out of me. She took a video of her face covered in cum and before she pushed it in her mouth and swallowed then told he husband that she had breakfast and to pick her up at the airport as scheduled.

I took one final picture of her laying naked on a trashed bed with that just fucked look. We showered together. I noticed a few battle scars (hickies) on her breast and thighs. She called them ribbons for a good time that she was sure her husband would ask about .. We dressed kissed and she returned to her room to pack and leave.

Saturday I got an email saying everything was fine at home. Wanted to know if it was ok to keep in touch via email till the next conference. She attached all the pictures.

No I won't forward the pictures as they are not mine to share

# 35. Soap gets in your eyes

My husband and I were invited to my mum's for dinner on Saturday evening, we were all chatting and the time flew by and after
a few more drinks we decided to stay over in my old room.

In the morning we had things to do at home, so I told Mike to
have first shower and I would follow him shortly.

But I was really shocked as I walked in, to find my young step-
sister, Julie, was kneeling, naked on the floor, in front of the
open shower door, soaking wet and she had clearly just finished
sucking my husband's cock.

I stood there with my mouth open in surprise, he was still
covered in soap suds and, when he saw me standing there, he
looked down in shock to see who had been servicing his lovely
manhood.

"I thought it was YOU" he gasped, but she just giggled and she
stood up smiling at me.

Just then Mum called up from downstairs
"Breakfast is ready" but Julie just licked
her lips and called back "I just had mine"

I wanted to slap her, then I realised that she was still gently cupping his balls, and I pulled her away and she just giggled as she
shrugged my arm off me and pranced out of the bathroom. still
naked and dripping wet.

I ran downstairs and sobbed in Mum's arms, but she told me it
was no big deal, she said Mike probably had soap in his eyes, and
didn't realise it wasn't me, and she said Julie was a kind loving

girl and she probably just saw a cock that was in need of some attention.

The thing is, I was hurt, but it things had been the other way round, if I had told Mike that I had sucked another man, he would say I was wonderful and that I had been a good girl.

Julie is not really very bright, but I think she is stunningly pretty, with shoulder length dark shiny hair, and huge brown eyes, and a proper size 12 woman figure.

I am a skinny size 10 and I have always been a little shy of my small bust, but hers are a firm, proud 36b and they jiggle so prettily as she walks round the house naked. She is almost always naked at home, and her neatly trimmed pussy patch
only seems to be there to frame her pouting, plump little cunt lips

Mum said I should not worry about Mike, she said perhaps he simply needed more attention, but we almost always make love every night, and Saturday night was almost the only time in ages that we were too late to bed for sex

Mum said in that case I should have asked him if he needed sex that morning, or at least I should have slipped under the covers and given him a loving suck to help wake him up.

I didn't really like being made to feel guilty like that, but she said Julie was only being a good girl and that she didn't have any intention of upsetting me, or trying to take my husband from me

But I can't stop thinking of his lovely cock
(MY property) in her sweet sexy, pouting little lips, and he neatly manicured hand tightly holding his love balls,

# 36. Coming soon!

My wife is shared, and has a guy that she gets with when they can, she does not "sleep around", she likes me, and him.
Today he sent an e-mail to me, expressing interest in a three-some sometime soon.
I asked if he had contacted her, because it's her call really.
He said he was about to send her something.

I text her "someone is about to e-mail you"

I responded to him that I was , of course, " ready for whatever they had in mind"

They did not disappoint.

We have a house in town (we live in the country), where we meet him when everyone's schedule allows.

He sent her a message saying that he would like for me to wait downstairs on the main floor, and that they would go up to the bedroom, where he intends to lick her to several orgasms, and then fuck her sweet pussy to a few more, and that when he is ready to cum, he would like for her to use her strap-on on him, while I suck him and take his load , then he would like to watch me kiss her with my cum filled mouth while I take my turn in her, and fill her.

My response?
yes, yes, yes, yes....

she text me that she will let me know what they decide.

Yes, I am hard.

We have been married many years, and have a great life, she and I.

I am certainly a 'cuck' in the sense that I share my wife, and, in it's purest form, cuckoldry does not exclusively include humiliation ( a surprise to many I am sure )

We role play many scenarios together and with others, but not so frequently that it loses it's charm.

I am what I refer to as "try-sexual", meaning I love sex, I have had no boundaries in the sexual arena since I was very young, I believe that limits have their place, but I have very few.

I became active ( sexually ) in 1969, and never looked back, through the sexual revolution, orgies, free love, groupsex, bi sex, sharing, cheating, watching, and being watched. I have been bull and cuck, side cock and sissy.

I love women, especially my wife, and all the wives and girl-friends before her.

I have reached an age where I do not have the stamina or desire to "cheat" with other women.

To be truthful, I have a dream wife, what would I be seeking other women for?

I like to fantasize with her and alone, I love it when other men share their wife pics with me (of course ) and I still Jack regularly.

While I accept the role of 'cuck' in certain scenarios, I am really just a pervert that loves sex, loves to see my woman pleasured in every way, regardless of who, or what that involves, I have no jealousy in my bones, and never have, I shared my girlfriends willingly from the very start.

I am sure after some of you get halfway through this you will want to express your disgust for bi activities, it's a waste of effort, move on if it isn't your cup of tea.

I like it all.

And no, I won't be sharing pictures, I only share what I have her approval to share, I would expect this courtesy from her as well, although she has never expressed an interest in sharing my pics with anyone....

# 37. Slut wife plays

Well this happened about 2 weeks ago and I am just finding out about it now.

I work outta town a lot and come home on weekends and one Thursday my wife and her sister and her husband met at a local bar and started drinking, Well for a long time now her sisters hubby wanted my wife, well after the drinks had been flowing my wife and her sister were getting very drunk, and her sister was getting very flirty with a guy at the bar. Well long story short this guy went home with them, to our home and Sister in law and this guy went in one bedroom and he fucked her and my wife and Brother in law went in another and wife told me, "he undressed her sucking on her tits and went down on her, then she went down on him and getting him rock hard then he got on top of her giving her a very good pounding filling her pussy with his cum.

After that she fell asleep and when she woke the other guy was in bed with her and Sister in law and Brother in law were gone leaving this guy with wife(not a good idea) Well after wife woke up and seeing this guy in bed with her she was shocked, so she says but not enough to get up he rolled over and started playing with her and before long he was fucking her and fucked her twice before getting up and leaving,, I have to say I wasn't happy about what I heard even though my wife is a shared wife there are rules we always follow to keep her safe this is not one of them, but this time all turn out ok

# 38. Mom's got the itch

Not really a story, but a tale which has recently been unraveled to me and honestly I can't stop thinking about it and find myself wanting to know more. So, here is...

This is a true reference which recently happened over the summer and is about the undenying and inevitable lust between Mother and Son. I am hearing 2nd/3rd-hand information and tidbits from my wife who is a close friend with the woman *mom involved. ---- Long story short the woman whom I'm attempting to describe is around my wife's age, or a few years younger so let's call it ~44 and for anonymity's sake call her Mary. * It should be noted that my wife and "Mary" have nibbled on each other in the past and have explored some "personal-time" together although my wife says that neither of them are full on lesbo's. Mary is also married and having the mid-life humdrums in her marriage w/ her husband whom she describes as "unattentive to her needs & sub-par in the bedroom". - ouch! lol. Mary's son *call him "Jason", is a tender 22 yrs old and in the making of a Military Career or at least an enlistment.- All I really know about that... So, adding it all up, you may have guessed that the lust between them two when Jason returned home for his visit led to an uncontrollable situation of love and lust in the most unadulterated and taboo form. As a man, I know and although most men won't admit to it- we have all thought of our moms/sisters/Aunts/cousins in some perverted way and have j/o to the thought. And as a mature/married man myself I can also see that the very sexy and good-looking mother here- Mary has no-doubt had issues of her own which were crying-out to be used and pleasured in the most cardinal way. So, the result was/is that,... in plain English the son and his mom started fucking and putting forth a strong fueled sexual relationship- an awakening is how it was described to my wife when she told it. - Btw, my wife and Mary had a session of their own with 69ing, bathing tog, and dildo/vibes upon hearing all that was happening there.-I wish that I had got the full story and details but I'll tell it the best I can.

When I asked how this all started and came about, my wife said that her son just made an effort to be with her and to be attentive to what she was saying, adding that it was nice to have someone actually listen to her for once. As a man, I'm realizing that this young man had a plan to seduce his mother from long before he got home. - Kudos to him- my fucking hero and very well played. lol Mary said that the looks between them were noticeable and becoming more evident each time. She said that Jason would offer to rub her shoulders or her feet when they were alone or when she got home from work, but not when his dad was around. In the morning he would make her coffee before work and offer to make eggs or a bite for her to eat. Mary told my wife that she started to think about that and her son while she was at work and found herself getting stimulated. Adding that one morning Jason brought her coffee into her bedroom while she was half naked and getting dressed.- He did the "OHH, excuse me mom" bit and she had done the "cover-up" with her hands, but she said that she could see his eyes scanning her half naked body repeatedly. - I'm saying to my wife...What does that mean? Was she standing there with her tits exposed to him, was she putting on her nylons, pulling up panties... What!!!??? IT was at this time that I had to tell my wife how sexy all this was and that I had to know everything she knew about this! Actually, that's all I got out of her because after admitting to her that it turned me on she told me that it did her as well and her and Mary got physical to the details as well, with that I had to take my own dick out and beg her to suck on it as I was thinking about what she just told me. This is getting long, call this part one. It's on my mind just about every day now and I'm currently trying to get to watch this somehow and see it unfold in real time to get my visuals in spec w/out all the what-if's and substituting all the improv's of how I want it to play out.

# 39. My wife

Hi, my name is Tony, and my wife's name is Evelyn. There's nothing special about us. We are in our sixties now, and this happened when I was 32, and my wife was 25. I was working for a large Agricultural estate in Northumberland near Ponteland. My wife was a housewife. We lived in a house provided by my work. Many times we had to get the estate joiner to some repairs to our house over the four years we were there, and I had got used to seeing the estate van parked outside our house when I was passing by on one of the tractors. I often used to joke with my wife about the "action" I was missing while he was there. She used to laugh about this

I was off work sick for three weeks because I had inhaled some insecticide while spraying when I got my redundancy notice, the estate was bust. Three days later the estate jointer turned up when I was at work, to replace a window frame, and when my wife told him we were going to leave he asked her to go out with him for a drink, but she said she was uncertain about how I would take it. My wife said about how I used to joke about him, and about him being her "boyfriend", and that she would have to ask me, before agreeing to go out with him.

When I got home for lunch that afternoon my wife said "After lunch, I have something to ask you" So after lunch was finished she came and knelt beside me on the floor and said "Jon fixed the window frame........and asked me out for a drink" I said "What did you say ?" She repeated what she said but added "and he didn't ask you. I told her to go for it and I would look after our two kids (one had just been born 8 weeks previously), to save trying to get à babysitter. I told her to enjoy herself, she needed a break. We had heard tales from Jon about other females he took out, even though he was married. The next day she phoned him and agreed to go for a drink at the hotel where he worked part time.

The day he was taking her out arrived. She wore a floral dress flat shoes, and she looked gorgeous. She said "Don't worry, nothing going to happen, he's not my type" He arrived at 7pm and when he came to the door I let him in. He was cheerfully, but nervous. They left at 7.30pm, kissing me before saying "Nothing is going to happen" I said " If it does, it does. I am not going to blame you. I got my eldest daughter straight to bed and fed the baby then settled down to watch TV. I must have dropped off to sleep and was woken when the phone rang about 11pm. It was my wife saying that they were heading home and should be about half an hour

11.30 came and went, no Evelyn. I fell asleep again and woke up when a car drove past. I got up to look out the door to see a car turning behind a street of houses that had been converted to garages. About 2.30am this car came back down the road and after a few minutes my wife came in the door

She gave me a kiss and cuddle, but she smelt different, more sexy. So I asked her if she enjoyed herself. "Oh yes", she said, then came to sit next to me on the sofa. She started to kiss me, and after a few minutes she took hold of my hand and put it on her pussy. It was hot, and very wet and sticky. I said "Has going out with Jon got you turned on?" She said "Put your fingers inside and feel how hot I am !" so I inserted my index finger, but she said "Give me more!" so I inserted both my middle and the next finger into her, but felt no resistance, so I tried with 4 fingers. It went in easily, and when I took it out, I looked at my hand. It was covered in white, sticky stuff, so I lifted her dress and checked her pussy. It was swollen, and covered with the same stuff that was on my hand. Then she told me. She said "He fucked me" then she added "I let him fuck me ,I couldn't resist it."

# 40. My wife 2

When my wife arrived home that night she was very excited. When she settled down she said "I've got something to tell you"
"John fucked me"
I was shocked! She had been so insistent that she had no intention of doing anything like that, so I asked her what changed her mind.
What you read next is my wife's story.
We went to the hotel where he works part-time; it's about 15 miles away. We went into the bar and John ordered drinks for us. I had a Tequila Sunrise as I knew that I was not liable to get drunk on those. He introduced me to a few of his friends when were there then we found out there was a dance at the hotel that night, so we went into the room where the dance was held. The room was dimly lit, except for the dance floor.
We had about 3 dancers before we needed another drink which I bought. When I returned to the table there was another couple there, and John had to move close to me. When he moved he put his hand on my knee, which I wasn't against. After a while I had to go to the toilet so I told John where I was going. He gave my knee a squeeze before letting go of it. When I got back to the table he'd bought more drinks and we got up to dance more. The band started to play a slow number, we were face to face when John put his arms around me tightly and kissed me. I was shocked, but it felt nice, so I didn't pull back from him. After a couple of minutes his hand was on my ass, squeezing very gently. He asked me if I minded, I said no; carry on, because it felt good.
We had more drinks, and more dances, and while we were dancing John was holding me tight and pressing his crotch into my

stomach, while groping my ass. The dance finished at 11.30pm and during the last dance I let my hand slide between us to where I could feel his cock. It was massive! At least 9" long, and very thick! I was thinking "would it fit? Would it be too big?" yours is only about 7" and reasonably thick. And that feels tight. John said to me "Happy now", I replied "Yes, very". Good he said. We then left the hotel to drive home but on the way back John asked if I minded if we parked up somewhere for a kiss and cuddle, I said no, but why don't we wait till we get back home and we can park behind the garages and you can kiss me all you like there ?Ok he said and we drove home. When he was driving home he put his hand on my leg and asked if I minded, I said no, and that you did it all the time. When we got back home we drove straight up past our house to where the garages are and pulled up around the back where it was very dark.

John put his arm around my shoulder and kissed me gently, I kissed him back. We were kissing for about 5 minutes when John said "Do you mind if I feel your tits?" "I moaned no!" He felt my tits for about 10 minutes and then stopped. I asked him "why did you stop?" he said that he was getting too carried away. I said "I'll tell you when I'm not happy with what you are doing" and grabbed hold of his cock. He froze, and said "What about Tony, will he not mind?" I said "Tony said I have a "hall pass" and can do what I like tonight, are you up for it, or not". "Hell yeah" he said.

It took him 5 minutes to get rid of his trousers, and I went straight down on his cock, slipping the head in my mouth about 2" with my hand around the base, hmmmmm. I moaned. He tasted wonderful.

After about 10 minutes he said "Your turn, get in the back seat". So I did and stretched out along the seat. He lifted my feet up to my shoulders and started to eat my pussy. God, it felt amazing. I had never had my pussy eaten by a man with a beard before. It tickled, but was exciting at the same time. It wasn't long before my pussy started to tingle and I told John "Put it in my pussy, put it in deep, make me cum on your cock !" When he came up from my pussy he got between my legs and put his cock head into my pussy then stopped. I said "why have you stopped?" he said "I don't want to hurt you" I said "I just had a kid 8 weeks ago so you're not likely to hurt me, just put it in deep. PLEASE". So he rammed it balls deep, it felt beautiful. He kept ramming me for 2 minutes till I came with an orgasm. He kept fucking me to another orgasm and then asked me where I wanted his cum as he was getting close. "Cum in me, cum deep in me" I screamed. "What if you get pregnant?" he said. "Tony will be fucking me when I get home, so he will think it's his, so cum in me". John fucked her for about another hour, making her cum again, and he once more before she came home thoroughly fucked.

# 41. Mom's got the itch 2

Ok, so continuing from what I said already, Jason was home for less than ten days his mom told my wife, in which time he had already seen her partially naked and was in the habit of asking her for coffee or breakfast when he knew there were good odds of seeing something. She said the frolicking between them was becoming more flirtatious by nature and that when he touched her, hugged her, massaged her neck or toes, the truth was that it was making her wet and horny thus giving her these type of thoughts she never had for her son before. Mary had told my wife that the first time Jason put his hands on her to caress her neck and shoulders he sat behind her and she could feel his penis harden into her lower back and ass/hips as he sat behind her and "gently caress me with his large hands" while pretending to watch T.V. together and small talk. - The truth was that when his dad/her husband pulled up it ended quickly and Mary said thank-you, telling him that "It felt so good to be pampered". - Nevertheless, Mary told my wife that she went into the bathroom, started up the bathtub and masturbated to more than a few orgasms in which she admitted about thinking how sex with Jason would be. *Upon hearing that from my wife I was like fuck that's hot- I knew she wanted it!mmmmm I told my wife what the ladies already assumed,- that there was no doubt he went to jack off a big load thinking about his mom at the same time she was doing it(to him). Her poor stupid husband, lol sorry, had/has no clue what was transpiring in front of him with his own family. I mean most guys prob wouldn't know much if their wives at least covered up her tracks a little bit, but how many husbands even consider that leaving your woman alone with her own son would ever amount to a lusting of infidelity and to go even further; incest under optimal conditions wanted by both his wife and his son?- I mean home with the family is the place to let your guard down,-A safe-zone if you will. Not for them, it was big-time fuckery and desire between a hot mom wanting a big dick from her son making his appearance as the new man of the house and it was a tremendous amount of sex-ual/incestual tension emanating from the both of them. It's gut wrenching to even pretend to be the cucked husband/father to say the least!...if you ask me, and the ladies it's best he never learn of the betrayal. Mary said "he has no idea" and that he doesn't get hard anyway..."

Upon further inquiry my wife said that Mary oddly felt wanted and needed by Jason's commitment to indulge her, though her mind would constantly remind her "This is wrong, WTF R U Doing?" etc- she was confused and left wanting more to say the least. Mary said that the flirtation between them picked up quickly and she herself knew that she was inciting these flirta-tions and temptations to grow further- to escalate. Mary said that she was wearing more provocative clothing at home when Jason was present-from which I understand was pretty much constantly. She would make an appearance at night while he would be up and they would play the forbidden-game together and sip drinks and watch television. She said that Jason one night prepared their drinks in just his tight underwear and a lit-tle cut-off shirt and she could clearly see the outline of his big cock bulging inside his underwear behind the fabric as he walked the drinks up to his mother's eyes on the couch.- It had to be like "Here's my cock mom- it's all yours if you want it"- but that's my thought. Mary did say that she kept taking a peek at his dick every time she sipped her wine and she could tell it was big and growing- like he was positioning it towards her. She also said that it was really an act of God that they didn't fuck right there on the sofa that night, but that was the first time it was clear to her that Jason was showing off to her and wanting to be seen by her as well. Besides dressing to draw attention from one another, and flirtations, let's kick it up a notch or two to some actual sexual tensions boiling over into first action.- Sound good?- You know you're hard and it does. lol Btw, my wife would kill me if she knew I'm putting it out here in the open as I swore confidentially that I wouldn't tell a soul. - Let's hope none of them visit WL. lol Good cut-off point for the final act or two with the info I have. Hopefully close it out. As always I wish I had firsthand knowledge of this from my own eyes it'd be a lot more descriptive and less all over the place

# 42. 1st Meeting

My wife works in an office that has bases all over the country. They got a new sales manager and with my wife dealing with sales in her job she got to talk to him a lot.

Said she had seen his pic in the company board and she thought he looked quite fit. Over 6 months they chatted on the phone being a little flirtatious or as much as can be at work.

She went in 1 day and he turned up mid morning working from the office my wife was at due to a sales deal he had to tie down. She said he looked even better in person. All day she said her pussy was tingling looking at him, his soft accent and the way he looked and smelt was sending her into meltdown. They chatted he was in meetings then she was in meetings said she couldn't concentrate on much all day.

She was leaving work when she bumped into him coming from a meeting. They chatted and he asked if she wanted a drink later on. Said he had another meeting that was due to finish at 7 so if she wanted they could meet for a drink at the hotel he was staying at then maybe she could show him a few bars around the city before he flew back the next day. She agreed

She got home showered and was starting to get dressed. I was getting dressed for work as I was on nights. She was telling me all about him as she put on her tiny thong, holdups, skirt then black push up bra and a chiffon black blouse. I was hard but needed to go to work but told her I wanted to hear the following night when I saw her.

The rest in how she told me:

She went to the hotel at 7, pussy was still tingling and she had already had a play in the shower and orgasmed. She couldn't see him so ordered a drink and sat at a table. Got to 7.30pm and she got a text saying his meeting was overrun and he would be there by 8. She ordered another drink. Just after 8 he turned up, still in his work suit and with his laptop bag. He apologized and said he would just nip to his room shower change and be down in 20 mins.

My wife looked at him noticing he was looking at her tits through her top and suggested that she should go to his room with him as she had already been waiting over an hour for him. He smiled and they headed to his room.

They got to the room, he put his laptop and other folders on the table turned round and they just kissed. His hands were quickly on her ass and tits, unclipping her bra under her top. They stopped kissing she removed her bra but still with her top on, asked if he liked that look as she took off her skirt. Said he just kissed her again, hands under her top playing with her nipples.

He stopped and took off his clothes, she took off her blouse and thong, she said he was hard already and he was average size. She lay on the bed opened her legs and he was straight in there with his tongue, said she orgamsed quickly before asking for his cock inside her. Said he reached over to the draw and took out a pack of condoms but she said he didn't need them, said he didn't hesitate just dropped the pack and slowly pushed his cock in her soaking pussy.

She wrapped her legs tighter round him as he thrust his cock in and out after a few mins said he was going to cum before she could say anything he pulled out and cum over her tummy.

He cleaned up and wiped his cum off her tummy. Said they laid there and kissed and stroked each other's bodies before he was hard again. She sucked him till he was really hard before she got on top and lowered herself onto him. She was slowing fucking him as his hands were all over her tits, she loved her nipples squeezed as she is on top and he was doing that without her asking. She reached another orgasm.

She climbed off and told him to fuck her from behind, she bent over the bed but he told her to lay face down on the bed, she did and he opened her legs slightly before pushing his cock into her pussy, she said she moaned, it felt soo tight. He carried on like this for a few mins before turning her over, again her legs wrapped around him as he fucked her hard. She had already had several orgasms and was close to another when he said he was going to cum. Her legs wrapped around him tighter so he couldn't pull out. He moaned as he unloaded a full load into her pussy. She kept her legs wrapped around him until she felt him go soft and flop out of her.

They cleaned up chatted for a bit before my wife got dressed and got a taxi home.

Next day she saw him a few times at work and before he left they agreed next time he was down they should do it again.

# 43. Pimped

It's been a long time since I've been on here but this is a story I've wanted to tell for ages. I was furious at the time but it still gives me a bit of a tingle when I think of it. In my glory days when I was much older and wiser

When I was 19 I moved in with an older guy who was very much into bondage. He used to tie my hands to the head board and then fuck me and I really enjoyed it. We progressed to me being tied with a piece of cord to a hook in the ceiling of the kitchen. I would be blindfolded and wouldn't be wearing any underwear. He'd go out of the front door and come in the through the kitchen door about 10 minutes later pretending to be someone else. He would then touch me all over and take my skirt off and undo my blouse and play with my pussy and tits. It was soooo exciting that I'd be soaking wet.

These little sessions always ended up with me being untied and led to the bedroom where he'd fuck me silly. Whilst we'd be making love he'd fantasize about what it would be like for one or two of his mates to actually come into the kitchen and find me like that. The very thought got me incredibly excited and our love making would be awesome!"

Well to cut a long story short we decided to do it one night. I got tied up, Geoff went into the front room and after a few minutes one of his mates came into the kitchen and played with my body. He didn't get to fuck me. He left after a while and Geoff and I had amazing sex. Well, one thing led to another and over the next few months I was played with and fucked by a number of his buddies. I never knew who they were, and Geoff insisted that they never spoke which added to the excitement.

One evening he had two of his buddies come in and they played with me and had their wicked way with me on the bed. Only difference was that this time one of them broke the "golden silence rule" and told Geoff at the front door that it was the best 50 quid he'd ever spent. The bastard was pimping me out and I never knew! I moved out that very night and never saw him again.

# 44. Our first MFMM.

Liz, Joe, and I have been what we've been calling Quality Time every other weekend and at least twice a week at lunch for about a year and half when this happened in 2006.

Joe scored 3 tickets to the Angels vs. Dodgers at the Big A. Joe loved the Angels and Liz and I were Dodgers fans. He let us know that these tickets were a friend of his he plays basketball with at the gym and was tailgating if we wanted to go.

"Or would you rather have a pre game fuck" my wife tells him. 20 minutes after her sister picked up our kid, Joe was over with his dick in my wife's mouth. We took turns on her, each of us cumming in her. Liz dressed in her sheer bra, a tight Dodges shirt, light blue G-strings, and some shorts that showed off her amazing legs and Ass.

We made it to our seat right before the national anthem. We met his buddy, Mario was more our age, he was a lot like me just a bit more on the athletic side. Mario eyes went straight to my wife's nipples poking through her Dodgers shirt, The beers were flowing, and during the game we learned he had two kids and a wife who spent more time at her moms with the kids then at home.

After the game we had planned on shooting some pool. So after a Angels victory we headed off and met up with his family friends, He asked us what we had planned, Joe tells him and invites them, his wife told him to go that she would be at her moms with the kids.

So the 3 of us are drinking and playing pool. Mario was an easy going guy, he had us laughing most of the night. I've been watching him steal glances at Liz all day, had me already thinking of him fucking my wife. Joe had the same Idea, as he pulled me to the side and asked me how I felt about him joining us for some fun. Again I let Joe know that I was thinking the same thing but it would be up to Liz.

Various songs were playing, Liz would be dancing around the table, she would dance with me and then Joe when she came to him, she skipped Mario twice before he said " I would like to dance with a fine Mommacita too".

Liz was having a blast, she had came up and gave me a big kiss and whispered in my ear "I'm horny as hell, It's time to go". I ask her if she mind if Mario came along. First thing she asks me is if Joe is cool with it. I tell her to ask him.

Liz walked over to Joe, Pulls him down and whispers in his ear, He nods his head yes, my dick is rock hard as I watch Liz walk over to Mario, She says something to him and he looks right at me, I give him a thumbs up, he nods his head Yes, Liz came back to me with a wicked grin "Give me the keys Papi and give us 10 minutes before you guys come out", and they both walked out. Joe looks at me like WTF, "Liz wanted 10 minutes" I tell him. Joe's adjusting himself as we wait the longest 10 minutes ever.

We get to the car, the light turned on when we opened the door. and Liz was topless, Mario was going to town on her tits, Liz just held his head on a tit like a baby nursing as we got in. It's about a 15 minute drive home. I see Mario in the mirror, "I love sucking your wife's nipples"

I hear Liz "well let see what's been poking my thigh" A minute or two and my wife's head disappeared and Mario's went back. "She sucks a mean dick, right" Joe says. The car is filled of moans from Mario and slurping and gagging from Liz. Mario moaned out he's close, Joe reached back and held Liz's head down, "she swallows bro go ahead" he says.

Mario lets out a few holy fucks then yelled out "I'm fucking cumming oh fuck, fuck, swallow it bitch yea, yea" Liz sits back up, "your wife ever do that", "not since H.S, sorry about calling you bitch" Joe answers before Liz could, " She prefers married slut, naughty wife" then Liz interrupted him "when your cumming in me you can call me anything you want".

At the house we walk in Liz wants a shower, Joe had other ideas and spun her around and kissed her hard sucking on her tongue as he strips her shorts off. He bends her over the coffee table and slips his dick right up my wife. Mario was wide eyed, "I've been curious what he looked like hard" Liz is taking it and moaning out "he better not cum it's still early".

Joe just starts hitting it harder, Mario starts playing with her tits and she starts to cum hard, Joe looks at me "I'm cumming in your wife for the second time today." Liz is in the middle of her own orgasm grinding her Phat A$$ back on him as he fills her up. As soon as Joe pulled out I was in her, Liz was going nuts, her pussy was contracting, she's talking dirty, just before I was about to cum she turns her head and says "Mario's gonna fuck your wife's A$$ Papi". I came hard into her, 4th load of the day for Liz in her kitty, and one down her throat. Liz grabs Joe " Shower time, Joe came out, taps my shoulder your next, Liz soaped me up and tells me she can't believe she just did that and how turned on she was.
I sent Mario in, Joe and I are down stairs, 20 minutes later we hear the shower stop, It wasn't too long we hear the head board hitting the wall and moans from my wife.

I turn on the stereo, and we went up stairs to see my wife on her back, Mario had her legs back pounding my wife into the bed, her pussy was a mess, making sexy sounds as he fucked the cum out of her, As we walked in Liz moans out to Mario if he ever tried a DP. "No" Liz had him pull out and had Joe lay down, she impaled herself on him with a fuck that cock feels so fucking good. I'm looking at Mario; his cock is about my length but a lot more thicker than me, not as thick as Joe.

I use a bit lube in her A$$, Mario asked for the lube, Joe pulls out and tell him to fuck her a bit then slide up her married A$$. He pulls out and begins to try and get into my wife's A$$. With a deep moan from Mario and low grunt from Liz he slipped into her. He worked most of his cock into her before Liz pushed back and took it all, Joe Pushed himself back into her. Liz was in heaven. Once Joe started pumping up into her, Mario started two pump her A$$, maybe 5 strokes and he was filling her A$$, "yea baby give it to me give me that cum in my A$$ baby" He pulls out, I give him a wet towel and take his place, Joe and I got into a good rhythm, fucking her good for about 15 minutes when Liz went into a huge body shaking orgasm flooding the bed, soon Joe stops as deep as he could, I could feel his cock swell then throb, I could feel the heat of his jizz, that set me off and I unloaded a second load into her A$$. 5 loads in her kitty, 2 n her A$$, and one down her throat. I look at the time, A little after. We ordered pizza.

The 3 of us left Liz in our room, turned out Mario liked to smoke the sticky Icky also, so we lit another joint. Liz came down a bit later in her dodgers' shirt and boy shorts "You fuckers really filled both my holes", her red boy shorts already had a big dark spot from our juices.

She gives me a big minty kiss and sits between Joe and I with Mario on the lazy boy. I've got my arm around her massaging her boob and rolling her nipples. She moans "You know what you're doing to me" She was getting excited, " good thing you've got 3 cocks here to take care of you". Mario was telling us there's no way his wife would let him fuck her A$$. Liz let him know that he's the first guy in her A$$ since we've been married. Liz mentions how turned on she is and can't wait for the next round. Joe grabs her boy shorts pulls then off, my wife knows what's coming and spreads her legs for Joe. He got down on his knees and started eating out Liz. I start playing with her tits, Liz moans out telling Mario to suck on her tits. Liz was moaning she was close, You could hear Joe lapping up all our juices, slip a couple digits into her, she was bucking her hips as she came on his face. Once Joe came up Liz sat up and started kissing him, sucking on his tongue, when there was a knock at the door.

Pizza was here. Joe was hard (Viagra induced we later found out), Mario and I had Semi wood, so we asked Liz to answer the door, which opens into the family room of our condo , her shirt covered her crotch, so the only thing the old Mexican guy could really see were her big tits and thick nipples poking through the thin material, and 3 men sitting in there in nothing but underwear.

As soon as the door shut Joe pulls out his raging boner. Liz put the pizza down and sits right down onto Joe's cock, Joe pulls her shirt off, cups both tits and starts playing with them. He pulls her back, he leaves' het tits and grabs her legs and spread them, Mario was just fixated on the scene in front of him. Liz is moaning out how hard he is and how good it feels.

I couldn't help it, I got up, gave my wife a big kiss, knelt down and started licking, sucking, and nibbling on her clit. Liz cried out in orgasm, her juices were flowing; I could taste the saltiness from the previous loads.

I pull off, Joe let's go of my wife, She gets up goes straight to Mario and starts sucking his dick to solid erection. Liz got onto all fours, Mario took his turn as Joe stuffed his head in to my wife's mouth. Mario pulled out, Liz tells Joe to lay on the couch. She straddles Joe, but before she sank down Joe's pole Mario dipped his dick back in her for minute before pulling out and being replaced by Joe, he started to spread her used brown eye, I tell Mario go for it man. Mario eased his thick cock into my wife's A$$, as he slipped in Liz started cumming loud, I stood on the couch and fed her my cock which she eagerly started sucking. Mario went at it hard at Liz's pleading and soon was nutting in my wife's butt again, I came down my wife's throat, I sit back, I ask Joe how close he is to busting, "would you mind taking Mario back I'm nowhere near close" was his reply.

We had a slice of pizza as Joe was doing my wife doggy. That's how I left them, 30 minutes later or so I return, there's no music so I can clearly hear the bed and Liz crying out " fuck me Daddy with that big cock, fuck your pussy Daddy" I go up to the bedroom, Joe has her legs pinned back as he was in the push up position fucking the hell out of my wife.

My wife's begging him to cum, she can't no more. Joe sweating, I walk up and play with my wife's tits, Joe's slows and shortens his strokes, Liz is shaking her head back and forth crying she can't cum anymore and trying to kick her legs free, she was pinned down, I started sucking her thick nipple and slide my hand to her stuffed kitty and started playing with her clit. she covered her mouth with both hands, I'm sure the neighbors still heard muffled screams as she started gushing, Joe gave a few more hard thrust and finally came into her. Once Joe let her go she just rolled on to her side still trembling and passed out. Joe falls back and asked what time he had to split. I tell by 10am, (we had just started fucking at our condo, this was our 3rd time). We weren't expecting her sister till noon.

We had a CaliKing size mattress so there was plenty of room, with my wife in between us we feel asleep.

"let me shower first", is what I woke me, I didn't see Joe, I'm looking at my wife, then Liz gets pulled down a little and her legs go up and wide, " Papi you guys fucked your naughty wife good, my A$$ is sore as hell, nasty guy here is making it feel better" she says as Joe is eating my wife out. " Easy fucker my pussy is sore thanks to marathon man." Liz moans as Joe slides up and into her. Joe lays a big kiss on Liz, she's sucking on his tongue and vice versa, Joe pulls back and tells her "If I'm the nasty guy that ate your sloppy married pussy and you just sucked all the juices of my face and tongue, what does that make you" My wife didn't miss a beat, it really turned me on to hear say "The nasty wife that just fucked 2 guys with my nasty husband" she pulled him down and they were tongue wresting as he started long stoking her slow, she's was creaming, she was telling him to cum, Joe started picking up the pace and soon was pounding Liz, he fucked her through one orgasm and slowed down a bit but kept a steady rhythm, a few minutes of this and Liz told him to cum or stop so she can use the restroom, Joe stopped. Liz went to the Bathroom, we soon hear the shower and her calling for Joe.

It's only 7:30am so we have plenty of time. After about 15 minutes I took a look in and he was fucking her in the shower. I'm hard, they finally came out, Joe still hadn't nutted. I took shower, when I came out Liz was riding him slow, Joe pulls her down, Liz is juicing or it was last night's Jizz coating Joe's dick and balls. He spreads her butt cheeks, he slips out and I slip into her sloppy gapped pussy, I pull out and let Joe back in, then I slip into her pussy with Joe, Liz cried out " you mother fuckers, oh fuck you guys, oh fuck now you got to fuck me". it was like she hit her 4th wind. I could only handle about 10 minutes of this before I busted in her. Liz seemed to be riding one long orgasm,

Joe moans he's close.

I check the time on the phone and there are 3 missed calls from her dad, Liz is sliding off Joe and grabs his dick hard and strokes it and sucks on the head a bit before laying back down "fuck me till you cum and make it quick".

# 45. The early days

This is a simple story from when we started playing. Initially, we dabbled in swapping with couples but it soon became apparent she'd much rather have both cocks to herself.

One of the first times we did it was a night we stayed in a motel near the beach. We had been out partying and got back to our room about 2:00. We were both decently buzzed and decided it would be fun to open the drapes about a foot and think about someone watching us. This particular motel had a reputation of being a place where swingers stayed while in town and I suppose it was no secret to the locals. We'd been fucking for about 10 minutes when I noticed someone standing outside. I told her we were being watched and she turned her attention to the window. All we could really see was a silhouette until he stepped back into the light. He was dressed in a tank and gym shorts and slowly stroking what appeared to be a huge cock. I guess he saw us both staring in his direction and he turned to the side, showing off the length of his dick. When she saw it, she whispered "let him in". I went over and opened the door and in a flash he dropped his shorts and was between her legs. I'd say he was at least 9" but very, very thick. Girth was her weakness....she came constantly as he pounded her.

The whole thing only lasted about ten minutes. After he came, he slipped his shorts on and headed out the door. She later said that part of the excitement for her was there was never a word spoken, although I know his size played a major role. We replayed it many, many times through the years.

*******************************************

A guy with 9 inches gets a lot more invitations than a guy with 6 inches. Love the impulse fucks. When she's hot, she'll do things she normally wouldn't.

We were at a house party once and a younger guy with a big dick wanted to fuck her but because of his age she was hesitant. She was 40, he was 28. She had never had a big dick. I talked her into forgetting his age and going for it. It was good, she trembled as he slow fucked her, not rough but firm and steady. She admitted he was good and she had never been fucked like that before. The next day during lunch, we were out on the town, I asked her what she wanted to do that afternoon. Her reply was to give that big dick guy some more pussy if it was ok with me. And she did. There were about 10 people in the living room watching TV. They muted the TV to listen to her grunting and moaning as he again slow fucked her firm and deep. The bedroom door was open, some went to watch briefly but she didn't seem to mind or care. Normally, her fucking with an audience was not gonna happen but in the heat of the moment, she melted, gave it up and just went with it, not caring who saw or heard. It was all about getting that big dick.

# 46. THE WORD IS GETTING OUT

I have wrote about encounters with young's (20s) awhile back, now the wife claims she doesn't want to play with young guys but she sure attracts them and they flirt with her for sure. She has played with young guys and they enjoy fucking her. The last bunch were friends of the Grandkids that came over did some work in the yard for days and ended up doing her with visits repeating the sexual play with her. Well looks like word got around, as I warned her about. She was very sexual the guys that came buy that were friends of the Grandson, friends always came by to hang out with him and use the pool and barbeque,. The wife most of the time would go out and mingle with them say funny things, and wears dresses that show a lot of boob. This time these guys came by to hang out with Grandson who was working, mind you grandson as we know does not know about the guys wife has fucked. I'm sure he wouldn't believe them anyway. IF THEY did say something to him it would ruin a good thing. So the wife went into the bed room and changed to a white dress almost you can see thru and the buttons unbuttoned all the way to her solarplex, lots of cleavage, she is a full 44d nice plump looking tits. I let them in and offered to sit down. She came in and sat in front of all of them, I winked at her. She started to talk to them and got a little animated with her arms and legs. As she does, these guys are laughing, I noticed her right boob oreo was slightly exposed. I DIDN'T SAY ANYTHING, the phone rang she leaned forward getting up and her boob fell out and was hanging there in the open I know these guys saw the whole boob, she straighten up and tucked it back in like nothing was happening. I told her I'll get it, she turned around to sit and U could see her ass crack thru the dress she had no under wear. I'm about to cum in my pants. She sat and you COULD SEE HER RIGHT BOOB STARTING TO peek out again I didn't say anything. When she sat her legs were spread U could see a glimpse of her cunt. Man these guys were getting a show. She got animated again her right boob was now exposing the nipple she had to be not aware of the exposure, I was having a turn on time watching them see her tits and her cunt. I know they were looking, it was so obvious.

Grandson was not coming home till late at night, one of the guys said well we better get going, so I said to them your welcome to stay a little and I will order a pizza, they looked at each other than my wife and said sure, her tit still exposed, she said good. The wife said to me why don't you go get it, I knew what she was up to, so I called it in. I took off to go pick it up, around the corner when I came back I figured she would be in the bed room with them, when I came in they were still in the living room however the one guy was rubbing her shoulders, her dress was pulled under her huge tits with one guy in front of her pinching her nipples, and her dress pulled all the way up exposing her pussy, the 3rd guy across watching. When I came in the living room she said I asked him if he could rub my shoulders. She said you guys can go eat the pizza my husband will get the oil and you can give me that full body massage you promised. They all said no we can eat pizza after. She pushed her tits out and ran a finger across her clit and wiggled her upper body. When she got up to go to the bed room she left her tits out and down the hall she started to remove the dress we followed, you could see a wet spot on her dress. I slid the bed spread off went to get a bunch of towels and oil, they had her dress off and they couldn't keep their hands off her, they were all over her she just stood there they squeezed her tits jamming fingers up her pussy, and one guy kissing her. They all took turns sucking her nipples.

I can tell you there was going to be no massage. They all started to pull their clothes off she got on the bed on her back and spread her legs real wide. She then yelled out what about my massage? She said pour the oil on my tits and massage them, so the one guy did and squeezed and massaged them with delight. Her legs were still spread he slid down still massaging her ate and licked her pussy. Another fella slid her over so her head hung over the bed, preceded to stuff his cock in her mouth, she said with a full mouth don't cum in my mouth. She's really getting hot, g...d she looks sexy all stretched out cock in mouth being fucked, legs spread and all of them taking turns squeezing her tits, she gagged a little and told the other guys "fuck me" the one licking her pussy climbed up to her tits she reached down and stuffed his cock into herself, he pumped her and she started to groan, she said his cock was hard. Her tits were wobbling around the guy watching was grabbing her tits. The guy fucking her grabbed her oiled tits squeezed them while ramming his cock into her which she really enjoyed. She said again that he was really hard. About that time he let out a groan he was cumming in her, he pulled out and stepped aside the guy squeezing her tits climbed between her still spread legs slid his cock into her liquid flooded cunt and pumped her, the sound of his cock was so hot pumping in and out her watery pussy. The guy in her throat groaned and cummed she wasn't bothered because she was building up to a climax then she exploded with a long orgasm, she at least 3 strong climaxes she is multi orgasmic. She grabbed the ass of the last guy fucking her, yelled ram it which he did she had another orgasm long, then he cummed on her stomach some of his cum squirted up to her face, she had cum dripping out she yelled I said don't cum in my mouth. The guy fucking her mouth lay next to her and caressed her up and down her body mostly on her tits and her pussy we all talked for awhile, I saw his cock was getting hard and her legs were little by little spreading, her nipples were becoming erect she reached down to his erecting cock and caressed it she looked at him and said G...d your hard. She sat up and put it in her mouth and slid all the way to the balls held it there then pumped quickly. We are all sitting on the bed except me she told him to fuck her he climbed on her and rammed her she really spread and kept saying yes ..yes and let out a long groan he kept pumping her for 2 to 3 min and then she cummed again then he exploded in her. He fell against her all spent.

# 47. Naughty church wife

A few weeks ago my wife and I went to a swinger's party. Something we had talked about for some time. There was something about her getting shared that excited both of us, but being church people we also fought the idea.

So we go to this party sadly it's not great, not our type of people. Just one guy chats to my wife that I think maybe but nothing happens. We chat to several couple but my wife just doesn't feel it.
We leave towards the end of the evening a bit disappointed but both willing to try again.

Now this guy I mentioned we did swap numbers and last week he messaged me to say hi and chat. He said he enjoyed meeting us, especially my wife, wondered if he could meet us. I said I will have to check with her first.
As we chatted a bit more he asked about our evening etc. I said it wasn't great and sadly she got no action. He said well I wouldn't say no action. I questioned him. He said at one point he met my wife as she watched a couple making out. He chatted to her and as she watched he lightly touched her arm, then her shoulders. He said she didn't stop him so he continued and slowly slid his hand inside her top down onto her naked tits. No bra on. Said he played with her tits for a while as she watched the other couple fucking. He asked her to join him in another room but says she refused.

My wife hadn't told me about this but has now . Said she felt bad as I hadn't seen but she did enjoy it. I've told her not to worry I love it that she did that.

So another trio is needed I think but maybe to another party.

# 48. Still at it!!!

So we have been back to our motel room back for a few hours since the bar closed down, but before this, it all started as wifey was feeling frisky and wanted to go dancing and mess around a bit!

I tried to book room a week ahead but was solidly full for Saturday as this place usually is very popular and convenient to stay for a night because of awesome live bands and music and atmosphere in general!

Wifey was a bit disappointed we had to do a bit of driving back after the party which I felt bad about it, but I joked that she should dress really slutty and we might get lucky if someone just invites us to stay in their room ...lol

So we were set to go as I call wifey that we are getting late and might mis getting a table as she announced that she is coming down, I look up the stairs and see my beautiful wife dressed to knock out the world, she is wearing a black high cut dress very tight with an open side cut and nearly fully open cleavage that part of her perfect size melons are dying to come out with a pair of fuckme pomps, as she gets to the bottom of the stairs she does a 360 and asks me " you like it honey, do you think someone will invite us to their room ", anticipation was killing me as I muttered omg who could say no to that as she laughed and said " I've given kitty a Brazilian was and left it out of her cage for easy access honey " as she strolled away ...I was dumbfounded and just followed her to the garage with a raging hard on, I opened the door for her she could hardly raise her leg to get in as she raised her dress way above I can clearly see her freshly shaved kitty , I ran across as I got in the car she pulls my head and gives me a passionate deep kiss and tells me we should take care of that strain in my pants before we drive out , I barely lasted a minute before I busted my nuts in her mouth as she swallow the whole load till the last drop and then drove off !

When we got to the party was a huge line up to get in , like always single ladies no cover charge and ahead of the line , wifey suggest that she should go ahead and meet up later inside , so she can secure a table for us , I said great idea as she goes to front of the line and the bouncer lets her in , was about an hour plus before I could get in , so I texted my wifey that it shouldn't take long for me to get in as I was very close to being admitted , she texted me back and said she secured a table and a room and will be on the dance floor if I couldn't find her on our usual sitting area .

Finally I got in and went to search for my wife on our usual sitting area and could not find her , so I got me a drink at the bar and kind of search for her in the dance floor until I spotted her dancing with this young tall very good looking young man well within his 30s, she is dancing as he is all over her with attention and by the looks of it she is loving it , so a slow song come up , and most of the floor clears up as I can now see where she is sitting , I walk towards the table as she is sitting between this two very handsome young men as she looks up and is very excited to see me and introduces me to her new friends Terry and Dale , I pull up a chair and sit in front of them and started small talk as they welcome me ...

As we all converse and my beautiful wife is sitting between this two studs my mind just drifted away in anticipation what the night awaits as I couldn't even focus on what we were talking about , but nonetheless they complemented me for having such a beautiful wife and how hot she was ...my wife just screeched STOP IT and excused herself to the ladies room !

So here we are just the three of us , as they tell me they are from out of town and on business for the week and that they were very fortunate to meet a couple like us and thank me for it , they also said that they were staying in the motel and had a few rooms and could give us one so we don't have to drive back so I too can enjoy drinking with them ! I thank them and took the offer!

So the party continued and was now in full throttle , now am not much of a dancer as I was born with two left feet as for my wife she loves to dance as much as Dale and Terry ! Both of them took turns on dancing with her as I would see thru the crowed I can make out that both of them could not keep their hands of her as they would be grabbing her ass and fondle her breasts and even had her between them dirty dancing , was very hot and I can just imagine how wet she was ! A slow song came on and she pulled me to the dance floor as now is midnight and she has had more than enough drinks , we are dancing as she held me tight and starts telling me how both of them can't keep their hands off her , she tells me Terry was fingering her while she was between them and how Dale manage to push one of her breast out while dancing , she also told me that Dale kissed her deeply as Terry blocked me from seeing that and that both of them grabbed her hands and placed it on their hard cocks , my heart was pounding and she was breathing heavily as she tells me she can't wait to go to their room !

After the slow dance my cock was now aching inside my pants as we walked back to the table and both Dale and Terry laughed and said she is quiete something she has us the same way ....we all laughed as I suggest it's almost closing time and we should take the party back to their rooms !
We all stood up and wait for wifey to take her last drink as she and Dale walked in front of us , down the long corridor we go as we are all tipsy , as Dale holds my wife's hand and halfway thru they are in arms as Dale plays with her ass ...we finally get to

the rooms as they both open different doors but have adjoining doors on the inside , Dale walked in with wifey and I walked in with Terry , he tells me to get comfortable and feel at home , I thank him as he grabs me a drink , now he opens the connecting door and tries to open the secondary door as it's still closed , he knocks on it and it eventually opens as Dale is just with a towel and tells us to come in !

Could not believe my eyes , my wife was already with her dress up to her waist and top rolled down with her size 36 honey dews and kitty soak in full view and kneeling on a pillow,
We all laughed and didn't take long for us to loose our clothes , Dale had a nice cock at least a 7 inch and thick comparable to mine while Terry was about more impressive he must of been easy 8 inches or more and very thick as wifey barely got his huge mushroom head inside her mouth , we are all standing in front of her as she takes turns on sucking our cocks !

She finally stands up as Dale unzips her dress and Terry helps her out of it as she is in all her glory just with high heels , as she strolls away and crawls on all fours on top of the bed slapping her ass and inviting the boys saying "what are you waiting for " as we all lost our clothing in a second , Terry crawled between her legs and started devouring her honey pot as she is holding his head down and grinding his face Dale put his massive cock at he face as she desperately tried to engulf her mouth , slurping and sucking and her moaning like I've never heard before , I decided to just sit on the chair and enjoy the show ...was awesome !

The three of them look so hot , as I see my wife of 30 years being pleasured by this two studs , my cock is solid and aching , but I just stroke it as the show continues , Dale moves up to top of wifey as he guided his massive cock into my wife's pussy , as he teases her and she tries to push into him as wanting his massive cock in her , he holds her legs right up and she guides his cock with her hands into her as I have a clear view of his entry into her married pussy , with one steady push he is balls deep as she grunts and groans of pleasure as Dale takes the opportunity to shove his huge mushroom head deep into her mouth , Terry speeds up his pace as he is now pounding her merciless as all she can do is moan as Terry is force feeding her his manhood , she cums and cums so many times that after about of fifteen minutes of hard pounding Terry empties his man milk deep into her as he lets her legs go , I can see her well filled pussy just oozing with man juices , now Dale goes between her legs and starts to guide his cock into her , he is now bigger than I thought , I stood up mesmerized to see such a huge member go inside her , am stroking my cock as I see her taking bit by bit deeper and deeper inside her until finally he is balls deep , now she is moaning and in total fury as she is pulling him deeper with her legs , she has gone wild , Terry grabs her head and shoves his cock deep down her throat as she gags and Dale is pounding her even harder , I just couldn't stand anymore I came all over them ,had no control of myself.

I stepped back to the chair still stoking my cock as they got heron all fours as Dale continues to pound her hard and Terry force feed his cock , this goes for a while as she sticks up higher her ass as Dale is groaning he is going to cum , wifey meets his cock with every thrust as dale holds her ass and unloads his seeds into her womb , he just holds her with his cock deep inside her as she cums very hard as Terry also looses his load all over her face and hair as she collapsed on her belly ...totally spent , they are all catching their breath , as I roll her over and open her legs and go down on her as it's full of cum just eating her away as I climb up on her and go balls deep in one thrust in her well used married pussy , it didn't take long to loose my load I kissed her and climbed off her to get a drink !

We took turns till early morning I ran out of steam just crawled into bed and crushed out ...just to hear my slutty wife still being used next door just until a few hours ago ...

After a number of hours had passed , I woke up to get a drink as I took a quick peek next door as to see where my wife was , looks like they were all spent out as well and the three of them were sound sleep completely nude with my beautiful wife in between Dale and Terry ...what a seen ! she has cum all over her hair and face , I can see clearly all her love bites on her neck and breasts , she has a lot of finger bruises all over her legs and arms ,her pussy still oozing cum , I just got an instant hard on and wanked until I could relief myself , covered them up with the bed sheets dimmed the light had another glass of JD and hit the bed !

I woke very late Sunday to the sound of loud moaning , as I walked into the room I see Dale behind my wife just drilling her and Terry has her head held with his cock deeply buried down her throat , she pulls away her head and moans "good morning dear ....oh god " and rolls her eyes as Dale is drilling her hard and deep , Terry say good morning as well and Dale just turns and nods his head as he increases his pace , Terry says he is sorry they didn't want to wake me up for breakfast ant mine was on the table , so I sat down to have my breakfast in full view of the three of them at it !

My breakfast looked great , I took my time eating it and finally having my cup of java as Dale and Terry took turns drilling my wife , what a scene to see my beautiful wife being taken by this two young bucks in all sort of positions ...and I had a raging hard on and could not wait to join in.
Terry and Dale help my wife off the bed and she walks towards me as she is wearing nothing but them high heels on and and says " is this your fantasy dear ...are you enjoying it " all I could do was nod yes as she calls Dale andTerry over and tells them "fuck me like a whore , fuck me like a slut my hubby loves it " as Dale bends her over holds her waist and drives his huge member balls deep in one stroke as she screams in delight as Terry quickly grabs her head and drives his cock deep into her throat , Dale is pounding her so hard and starts getting very ver-

bal calling he a slut and a whore , slapping her ass cheeks asking her to stick up her ass higher as she obliged , I can't believe how hard she is getting fucked while am still having my coffee , my cock is just raging for relief , Dale grabs both her hands and now is pulling her towards his huge member as I can see up close he is bigger than I thought , he goes deep and long and faster and faster as my wife is now begging for more , Terry now has her by her hair as he is fucking her mouth as well and he too is going deep as she gags and moans at the same time , Dale tells her to stick her ass up like the whore she is , I can see my wife raise her ass higher and higher as Dale drills her harder and faster and screams am cumming as my wife pushes against his cock and he holds her tight and empties his nuts deep inside my wife until he is limp and pulls away ...

I can't believe it happened a foot away from me , my raging hard on is killing me as I stand up go behind my wife and go balls deep in one thrust , she is so loose and wet , her pussy is just oozing with cum as I pumped her swishing sounds of her well used pussy I hear , I fuck her nice and slow as she still has Terry's cock in her mouth , she throws her hand behind her ass cheeks and opens it up as I am pumping her slow enjoying every bit of her , looks like she is loving it too as she asked me to pump her harder and give her more , I took my time as she became more desperate to use her harder and started telling me "do you like how they used your wife ...they haven't stoped using your wife yet ...fuck my used pussy fuck me harder please " I couldn't take it anymore and finally she screams out " fuck me fuck me like those studs , fuck my unprotected pussy , give it to me , fill me up , shoot it deep into my unprotected womb fuckkkk meee pleaseeee " , I see Terry sneaking his cock down her throat each time he had a chance and then cummed all over her face and hair , as for me I grabbed her hands and pulled her even harder and unloaded deep inside her already full unprotected womb ...held her there until I was limp she turned around hugged me and gave me a gentle kiss and said she is going to take a shower if anyone is interested and walked away still wearing her high heels ....

As my wife walked away they are just dumbfounded as how she can take so much cock and be able to just walk away with a prance as literally not even hurting after an entire day and morning of some serious screwing , Dale and Terry are mesmerized by the fact that even at this point she is unsealed after her pussy being pounded so hard , both of them tell me how lucky I am to have such a hot wife and that they wished their spouses would be like her !

While she took a shower with the door open we can all see her cleaning herself giving us a super show as she bends down soaping herself every crack and crevice , Dale stands up and says such a waste of water I might as well take a shower too as Terry and I laugh , but by the looks of Dale his cock is already in full atención as he walks into the oversized shower stall and joins my wife , they embrace in a hug as Dales cock pokes her love hole with his big member as she tries to avoid it and sticks her ass out , he is caressing her breast and ass while she gently strokes his now huge member , this goes on for a while as she gets pushed down on her knees and she quickly takes care of his love stick , barely fitting inside her mouth she desperately tries even harder , she stands up and are locked in a hug as she steps out of the shower and walks back towards us and has a huge smirk on her face , she crawls on top of the bed as Dale followed she looses her towel , Dale dives for her honey pot as Terry and I just stare at them going at each other like two wild animals in heat , wifey pulls him up as she opens her legs grabs his massive cock and guides it inside as she purrrs like a kitten in heat as he shoves it in , she raises her legs even higher and starts to pant and shake as she encounters another huge orgasm , we can see from our table her glistening love hole with this bucks seed , he turns her around and now she is on all fours as he smacks her ass and asks her to raise her ass nice and high as she quickly obliges him as Dale is now rubbing the presumed on my wifeys anus , Terry and I are just staring how amazing they both look , Dale quickly drives his huge member inside her with one thrust as she puts her head and chest and moans as he pulls it out and drills herw pushing against it as she is now screaming it's to big it's to big , he holds his prick and picks up more pre cum of her pussy and I determined to go in , Terry asks me if she enjoys anal , I tell him yes and the reason I haven't haven't told them was cause I wanted her to ask for it as she has many times turn down if she is not in the mood !

Wifey still with her ass high in the air is wiggling trying to get Dales huge mushroom head into her as he pushes his member firmly with his hands finally popping it's head inside causing my wife to give out a loud groan ,she is grabbing the bed sheets in pain and pleasure at the same time ,as she further wiggles her ass to accommodate his cock as it is slowly invading her most inner parts of her cavity , Dale is just holding her ass cheeks as wifey keeps on pushing against him until he is half way inside as he now starts slowly thrusting his love rod deeper and deeper with each thrust it takes about 10 minutes for her to get accustomed to his size and she is now the one that is pushing faster and deeper as as Dale pumps her brown hole ...now she has been completely used as a hot wife that she has been since married !

What a view Terry and I have we are both stroking our cocks as we see her getting pumped merciless , Dale gets off from his knees and goes into a squawk position and pumps her even harder as wifey screams of joy could probably heard across and down the hall way , he doesn't stop drilling her until he is just about to finish deep in her , as he grabs her by the hair and gets very verbal asking her to lift her ass like the whore she is , as she obligesby doing so , calls her all types of names until he blows his nuts deep into her forbidden hole ....they both collapse as Dale rolls to the side and holds my hot wife in his arms and tells her she is the hottest woman he had ever had ....

# 49. The AWAKENING 2

After my surprising afternoon with Annie I drove home and fixed a drink and slipped into a hot bath. I had to think about where I could take this highly sexed senior citizen. I kept running the events of the day thru my head wondering what's next.

Two days later I got a text from Annie asking me over for coffee.
I knew that was probably code for hot sex.
Stopped by an adult toy place and picked up a 10" rabbit.. Let's see if she could keep up with that.. If so she might like a threesome with an 11" cock to enjoy.

I rang her doorbell and Annie answered in what looked like her Sunday best.
I gave her a non sexual hug and took a seat at the table putting the toy on the table away from her.. We chatted about tame subject matter.
Then suddenly she lowered her head and quietly asked if I had enjoyed my last visit.
Her face lit up when I told her it was a great visit.

I leaned over and gave her a gentle kiss hoping that would get me an invitation to repeat our previous day's events.
Annie grabbed my hand and led me to the living room and we sat on the sofa.
Instantly she was all over me like two teenagers in a heated embrace.
Suddenly she stops and stands in front of me in a dress with buttons all down the front. She reaches up and begins to unbutton it all the way down shrugs it off her shoulders and strikes a sexy pose in a black lace bra and panty set. "You like? I went to

Victoria Secrets yesterday and bought this just for you"
I got up and got the rabbit and gave it to her.. Like a kid at Christmas she was in aw at the possibility of pleasures it would give.
I undressed and escorted her to the bedroom.. Standing next to the bed I embraced Annie and kissed her deeply.
I unclasped her bra and admired the beauty of her 34b breasts. Here's an 85 year old woman but her body is smooth and tight and begs for me to lick and kiss every inch.
While I kiss her bare chest I begin to slide her new panties down and off.. My lips follow down to her vagina covered in a small bush where her lips are throbbing and begging for attention.
I surgically run my tongue all thru the Busch searching out her erect clit.. I bite it gently and Annie is in full orgasm.
I stand up and push her shoulders down to put her on her knees and my penis is pointing to her mouth. Without a word Annie opens her mouth and tries to swallow me.. I was able to fuck her throat until she starts to gag.. I pull out and begins to fuck her mouth.
Annie is drooling dripping on her hard nipples and sucking my dick

I pull out and have her lie on her back and I lay on top of her using mouth to lick, suck and nibble on almost every inch of her body.
My fingers slip inside her pussy as her back arches.
I pull the rabbit out of the box and run it between her pussy lips to get it wet. She is dripping. I decide to spank her pussy with this large black fake penis. Sensations spread to every nerve ending in little Annie's body. I lean over and kiss her deeply and she eagerly sucks my tongue. While kissing her I slip the rabbit into her honeypot. I hold her so she can't stop kissing while I start pumping this
11" vibrator deep into her body.
She's hugging like a vice. I turn it on and the vibrator is touching every inch of her pussy... I moved down and started eat her pussy and licking her ••••••• getting good and wet and I slowly in-

serted the rabbit while I'm eating her pussy... I can feel the rabbit Vibration in her ass and moved up and in one stroke buried my dick balls deep in this shy demur little lady turned hot slut. I start pumping my dick hard and fast and the rabbit is reaming her ass. Annie is screaming as orgasms rack her continuously and I'm sucking her tits. My full balls begin to blast her pussy full of cum and as I do

Annie passes out and I am spent.

I take the vibrator out of her and turn it off.

I sit up and look over her body and see her breathing hard lying there satisfied and unconscious.

I grab my phone and get a couple of pictures especially the cream pie dripping from her gaping pussy.

Hmm how can I top this?

How about a threesome.. I wonder if I could get this church lady to eat pussy?

# 50. My wife (leaving party)

So we arranged the party two weeks after John had fucked my wife on their date night. We had told everyone to be at our house for 7.30pm. People started arriving from 6. 45, I was in the kitchen mixing punch when my friends wife arrived with the news that Gordon, my friend for the past 4 years, and darts team captain, would not be coming as he had the flu.

By the time 8.15pm had arrived everybody was here. Some were dancing, others were just sitting around talking. John had arrived last , apologising for being late, he was looking very sheepish, and tried to avoid me. I called him into the kitchen and shut the door behind him. I said " John, Eve's told me what happened when you took her for a drink, and you have nothing to be scared of. I dont mind, she's never been happier. He heaved a sigh of relief.

After a while the party started to liven up somewhat, the music got louder, the dancing got closer, and I was in the kitchen mixing more punch when Mary came in and closed the door behind her. She walked up to me and putting her hand on my arm, she said " I dont know if you have seen it but John has his hand on Eve's ass, and he's feeling her up !" I said "She's a big girl now, if she's not happy she will tell him to stop". When I went back into the sitting room they were sitting on the sofa, side by side. John had his hand behind my wife. I gave John a wink and he relaxed a bit. My wife came up to me and said "we have to speak) and walked into the kitchen, I followed and closed the door.

She said " Wait until everybody except John has gone then I'm going to feed the dog, and then I'll sneak into the bedroom and you can ask John into the bedroom to look at the window frame, tell him the window wont open, I've got something to give him so that he will remember us, it's something special". At 11.00pm everyone except John had gone home and I had made a coffee. We were sitting drinking it and John was trying to apologise to me again about what had happened with my wife, when I heard her call from the bedroom. I said to John "Can you look at our bedroom window for me, I think it's broken the hinges ?" "Sure" he said and walked to the bedroom door, I followed. When we went through the doorway we couldn't believe our eyes. There was my wife laying on the bed, on her stomach, totally naked ! "See anything you like ?" she said to him. " Yes, but I thought you would have had enough the other night" My wife replied "I've got more than one hole John. I'm wet, strip off and come here.

He stripped in about 5 minutes and looked at me and said "Are you going to join in ?". I replied "I think it's you she wants. She wants you to remember her by giving you something special, Enjoy".

He walked to the bed and grabbed her ass and parted her cheeks until you could see her butt hole winking and he went down on her, licking her pussey from her clitoris to her ass hole. Sticking his tongue first in her pussey deeply as far as he could. She groaned "Yes John, Eat me harder" then after licking her clitoris a few times, he stuck his tongue up her ass as far as he could. "Arrghh, I'm cumming" she said. "Fuck me, Fuck me now !" He climbed up the bed a little and got between her knees. Lifting her legs up over his shoulders he placed his cock at her pussey. Before he could push to enter her, she seemed to lurch upwards and screamed "YES, OH YES, HE'S RIGHT IN" John started a slow rythem in and out. He was fucking her balls deep for about 10 minutes when she gasped "I'm going to cum again, Oh Fuck I'm cumminggggg" John started to speed up till he started the short strokes and I knew he was about to cum. "Oh Yeah, Yeah" he screamed "I'm cumming deep in your pussey" he said.

My wife got up and went into the kitchen for a drink. I followed and asked he if they were finished, " Hell no" she replied, "You know I love you and I always will" and she gave me a lingering

French kiss. 2Then she went back into the bedroom.

She went into the room and climbed straight up on John and kissed him. " I'm going to give you a blow job now to get you hard again, and then you can fuck my ass, if you can get it up again" She then went down on him and sucked him right in. He screamed. " You slut". She replied " Yes, your slut, I never fucked an other cock till I went out with you" She started to suck him deeply, going right to his balls. She would never suck me that deep, saying that it made her gag. Up, down she went, stopping at his pee slit with the tip of her tongue, hmmmmm she said " I love this cock" After about 10 minutes she said to John "Get the KY out of the drawer and lube my ass with it" which he did. She got on her knees in front of him while John plastered a good amount o KY on her ass and spread it around. Pushing some of it up into her. Then he gave a liberal coating to his cock. She knelt down with her head on the pillow and said "Give it to me now, I want your cock in my ASSSSS". He put the tip of his cock to my wifes butt hole and pushed. It slipped away and she shouted " Aarrgghh, put it in before you push !" so he got hold of his cock and pushed gently. His cock head slipped in, then she told him " Stop pushing and let me get used to its thickness". After she had a little time to get used to it she started rocking backwards onto his cock, each time going a little deeper while moaning "God, this is good" and "Fuck me, Fuck my ass, Fuck me up the ass". Then she suddenly let out a yell, " I'm cuummmming". It was the first time that she had ever cum while getting her ass fucked. John started to build up his speed, slamming into her full depth of his cock and when he was near to Cummings he said "Where do you want my cum, in your mouth, or up your ass ?" My wife screamed "Dont you dare pull out. I want that cum inside me as deep as you can get it".

The night finished around 4 am with her getting another 2 loads in her ass. We haven't seen John since but at least he got something to remember.